DANGER
in the Depths

The Shadow Creek Ranch Series

DANGER
in the Depths

Charles Mills

REVIEW AND HERALD® PUBLISHING ASSOCIATION
HAGERSTOWN, MD 21740

Copyright © 1995
Review and Herald® Publishing Association

The author assumes full responsibility for the accuracy of all
facts and quotations as cited in this book.

This book was
Edited by Raymond H. Woolsey
Cover design by Alan Forquer
Cover illustration by Joe Van Severen
Type set: 11.5/13.5 New Century Schoolbook

PRINTED IN U.S.A.

99 98 97 96 95   10 9 8 7 6 5 4 3 2 1

R&H Cataloging Service
Mills, Charles Henning, 1950-
    Danger in the depths.

    I. Title.

                813.54

ISBN 0-8280-0982-1

Dedication

To Dorinda

My light in a dark world.

Contents

CHAPTER 1

Silent Scream

"Where is she?" Mr. Hanson shouted across the churning waters. "Joey! Where's Wendy?"

The boy on the shore calmed his powerful, black horse as the floatplane taxied in their direction.

"She went for help," he called, trying to be heard above the roar of the aircraft's engine. "I told her not to. Honest. She just left. Took Early. Snuck out of camp while we were still sleeping. You gotta believe me."

Mr. Hanson shook his head slowly, a deep sigh whispering past his lips. "I believe you," he said, even though he knew the boy on the shore couldn't hear. Turning to the pilot, he added, "Seems I spend half my life trying to track down one or the other of my two daughters. This time it's Wendy, heading off across the Bob Marshall Wilderness with nothing but her horse and dumb luck to guide her. I can guarantee you neither girl nor beast knows which end is up in this part of the country. We're a long way from Shadow Creek Ranch."

Hawk pulled the bright red mixture knob that controlled the flow of air to the carburetor and waited for the engine to sputter. As the blades clicked to a stop, the wings of the old Pacemaker rocked gently, momentum carrying the craft shoreward. "She thinks she being noble," the pilot said. "Eleven-year-olds tend to do that from time to time."

The Pacemaker's long, sturdy floats ground into the sandy bank as Joey ran up and grabbed a wingtip. "We'll find her," the man at the controls encouraged, his rough, dark-skinned features forming a hopeful smile. "After all, here stands young Joey Dugan. We've been huntin' him for two days!"

"Hey, Mr. H," the boy responded, his thick East Village accent lifting his words into the cool Montana mountain air. "You gonna sit there all afternoon or what?"

Mr. Hanson nodded and unbuckled his seat belt. Slipping back into the cabin, he unlatched the exit door and let it swing open. "Hi, Joey," he said, his voice sounding tired. "You OK?"

"Well," the boy grinned, "things are definitely looking up now that you're here. This ain't exactly been my idea of a picture-perfect camping trip, if you catch my drift. First our guide gets ventilated by a guy who kidnapped his own son, then Wendy and Early decide to play Lewis and Clark."

Mr. Hanson stepped off the float and walked a few paces along the shore. "Yeah, I heard. Ranger Perez found Jonathan Andrews south of here, drunk as a skunk." The lawyer's eyes scanned the mountain peaks and the nearby lush meadow ringed with trees. "Nice valley," he said.

"Beauty is in the eye of the beholder," Joey stated flatly. "Other than the fact that trail boss Parker left a few pints of blood in the meadow, and there just happens to be a .357 Magnum lying on the bottom of the river, it has its charms." The boy moved closer to his companion. "I hope the old guy makes it."

Mr. Hanson noticed Joey was shaking slightly. "You guys had a pretty rough time, huh?" he asked.

"Yeah."

"You OK?"

After a long pause, Joey spoke. "I told her not to go, Mr. H. I told her we gotta stay together. I was takin' good care of her just like you want me to."

Mr. Hanson placed a hand on the teenager's shoulder. "I don't blame you, Joey," he said softly. "Wendy's Wendy. We all know that. If she gets some harebrained plan in that stubborn head of hers, there's not much we can do to stop her. I know it wasn't your fault. Understand?"

Joey looked away. "There's somethin' else you gotta know," he said. "Wendy set out to follow this river. But this isn't your ordinary fishin' creek. Boss Parker says it's kinda weird. Indians named it the River of Fear. He says it comes and goes for no reason at all."

"What do you mean, it comes and goes?"

"Boss Parker says it can disappear without a trace, all of a sudden like—you know, puff, vanish into thin air."

"And you believe him?"

Joey shook his head. "Well, he was right about other stuff. Take this valley. He found it and it's not on my hiking map. Ditto the river. Makes you wonder."

"So, what do we do next?" Hawk asked as he joined the two by the water's edge.

Mr. Hanson pointed as he spoke. "Hawk, this is Joey. Joey, Hawk. He's the top ace of the tourist set down on Flathead Lake. Gives rides in his airplane. That's it over there. Called a Pacemaker."

Joey eyed the aging fabric-covered, high-winged monoplane wearily. "You must be one brave dude," he said. "You too, Mr. H."

The lawyer chuckled. "Hawk's a good pilot. Tracked you down, didn't we?"

"Now we just gotta catch up with Wendy," Joey responded. Turning to the pilot, he asked, "Can you follow a river from the air?"

"If I can see it, I can follow it," Hawk announced with enthusiasm.

"Then let's get goin'!" Joey called, running in the direction of his black stallion. "I'll tether Tar Boy in the meadow. He's been here so long he thinks he's home."

Hawk watched the teenager disappear through the line of trees that separated the sandy shore from the distant pasture. "Joey's got a lot going for him, doesn't he?" the man said.

"One of a kind," Mr. Hanson agreed. "But you should've seen him the first time we met. I'll tell you about it sometime."

"And I'd like to hear it."

Joey emerged from the trees and sprinted toward the Pacemaker. "I'm sure she headed west, toward the South Fork, following the river," he called. "If the route was clear, she could be halfway out of the wilderness by now. If not, she might be just over those hills."

Mr. Hanson and Hawk hurried to the aircraft and clambered aboard. "Looks like we've got a few hours of sunlight left," the younger man announced. "How's the gas situation, Hawk?"

"Half tanks. More than enough to poke around and get back to Polson for a fill-up. Young Dugan may have to camp out another night if we don't find anything."

"No problem," Joey chuckled, adjusting his seat belt. "Not a whole lot else can happen to me in this stupid valley. Me and Tar Boy will be fine. Let's just find Wendy and her horse before anything else goes wrong."

The Pacemaker was soon skimming the water, engine roaring. In moments, the valley was still once again, save for the fading drone of the low-flying floatplane.

The panorama of beauty that spread out below their wings captured the traveler's attention with delightful intensity. Mountains rose unencumbered from green valleys to rocky peaks. Meadows dotted the landscape, creating a random patchwork quilt of yellow and brown earth.

But one feature of the ever-changing vista remained constantly within view. It was the river, flowing blue and silver, following the contours of the wilderness, turning, twisting, dodging the occasional outcropping of rocks, skirting a sandbar here, a clump of fallen logs there.

The river seemed somehow a part of the landscape, and somehow not. As the Pacemaker sliced through the still air, the passengers noticed that the waterway began to have a mind of its own. Instead of turning aside for a natural barrier, it chose to plow through it. Instead of diverting itself around an outcropping, it flowed over it, turning into a white rage of tumbling, churning rapids.

Joey leaned forward, his head pressing against the window. "Something's wrong," he called, trying to be heard above the wail of the engine. "A river shouldn't do that. It's . . . it's unnatural."

"How 'bout it, Hawk?" Mr. Hanson shouted. "Is that normal?"

The pilot studied the scene below. "Can't say as I've ever seen a river act that way. Look down there." He pointed and banked the airplane to the left. "See? There goes the old riverbed. Cuts through the trees beyond that sandbar. But it's dry as dust. The river turns on its own. Heads north instead of west. But there's nothing there to make it alter course. No bank, no buildup of debris. It just turns."

Mr. Hanson's brow furrowed. "Are you sure this was the river Wendy followed?" he called.

Joey nodded his head. "It's the same one that flows out of Boss Parker's hidden valley. We've been trackin' it dead-on."

The Pacemaker rose slightly to keep above a lift in the land. As it topped the rise, all three occupants gasped. There was nothing in front of them but a deep green carpet of trees.

Hawk slammed his foot down on the right rudder and tilted the plane over on its side. The world swirled below; a vibrating wing pointed downward as if the Pacemaker itself couldn't believe what it was seeing.

"THE RIVER!" Joey shouted. "IT'S GONE!"

Mr. Hanson fought the overpowering force of the sudden turn, a force attempting to press him down against the floor. "Maybe it changed course. Maybe we missed it."

Hawk leveled the wings and lifted the nose slightly. Crossing the top of the ridge, the river suddenly reappeared, its surface boiling, seething, dark with anger.

"It can't be!" Mr. Hanson gasped, clawing at the Plexiglas window. "Where does it go? What happens to it?"

Hawk pulled back on the throttle and eased the plane into another turn. "I'll circle overhead, slowly this time. There's got to be an explanation."

As the pilot guided his noisy, trembling machine around for a third pass, Joey and Mr. Hanson pressed their faces against the window in breathless anticipation. The land began to rise slightly. Hawk lifted the airplane, keeping them safely above the trees, the wings straining to stay in the air at the reduced speed.

They saw the river twist and turn, its waters boiling like liquid in a hot kettle. Suddenly, the surface became a placid dark green. The next moment, it seemed the bottom of the land simply fell away, taking the river with it. They caught a glimpse of a huge, dark hole, with the entire waterway spilling into its featureless depths. Then the scene was gone, replaced by the serenity of a mountain forest.

As the aircraft skimmed the treetops, no one spoke. The vision they'd just seen was too fantastic, too bizarre, to be believed.

"Impossible," Mr. Hanson breathed. "Now I've seen everything. If Wendy makes it this far, she's going to get quite a shock."

He looked back at Joey. "Your trail boss Parker was right. That's one crazy . . ." The boy's face was colorless, eyes wide in terror.

"Hey, Joey," the man called. "It's just a freak of nature, that's all."

"Fly over it again," the boy whispered.

"What? I can't hear you."

"Fly over it again," Joey said, this time louder.

"Did you say fly over it again?"

The boy nodded, his hands trembling almost uncontrollably.

"Come on, Joey," Mr. Hanson chuckled. "This is no time for sightseeing. If we're going to find Wendy we're going to have to—"

"FLY OVER IT AGAIN! PLEASE!"

Hawk frowned. "Sure thing, Joey," he replied,

casting a concerned glance in Mr. Hanson's direction. "We can do that. Whatever you say."

The Pacemaker moved in a wide arc over the forest, filling the area with its mechanical song.

"Go slower," Joey said, his words almost lost in the whine of the engine. Hawk guided the aircraft once again until they were over the river, cresting the rise. The opening in the ground appeared up ahead, rushing toward them.

"There," the boy called, his voice shaking. "There on the bank, by the opening. Do you see it?"

Mr. Hanson scanned the site that Joey indicated. Fallen logs had been piled high by the rushing river, creating a temporary barrier just beside the spot where the waterway plunged into the darkness.

"I see a bunch of logs," he called. "See? There's nothing—"

The man's hand shot to his mouth as his words suddenly choked in his throat. Lying among the piles of twisted, broken logs was the still, unmoving form of a saddleless horse, one leg thrust upward, head back, mouth open.

The horrible spectacle lasted only a second before it moved out of sight below the speeding airplane. But it was long enough for Joey and Mr. Hanson to recognize the grotesque figure below as Wendy's horse, Early.

A scream rose soundlessly in the lawyer's throat. It was the scream of a man who knew he was looking into the open tomb of his own daughter.

* * * * *

Wrangler Barry heard the phone ring just as he was about to take the first sip of his favorite soup. The hearty aroma of hot vegetables and tomato broth tempted him to let the call go unanswered. But he knew Grandpa Hanson wasn't paying him to eat. His job was to look after the ranch and its livestock, and to answer the phone—even when it rang at the worst possible time.

Grabbing his ever-present cane, he hobbled quickly to the hallway and lifted the receiver. "Shadow Creek Ranch," he announced, savoring the inviting smell that drifted from the dining room.

The voice on the other end of the line poured out an unintelligible stream of words in a frantic attempt to communicate.

"Hey, slow down," the horseman chuckled. "I can't understand—" Suddenly he realized who was calling. "Debbie? Is that you? What's wrong?"

He waited in the quiet of the big Station's foyer, listening to the fear that drove the words of the unseen speaker. All thoughts of food vanished as the report flowed in from a distant breaking heart, a heart he happened to love.

"Debbie, listen to me," he interrupted, cradling the receiver in both hands in an attempt to touch the terrified caller. "You don't know if she's down there. You can't be sure. Maybe she fell off before Early was caught by the river. It's possible, you know."

He listened again, visualizing Debbie's loving, gentle face now creased and tear-stained with agonizing concern. The facts didn't look good. Wendy and Early had wandered off from their camp alone, following a river. Now the horse had been sighted at the mouth of a huge hole in the ground. Glancing out the front door, Barry could see that the sun was setting, halting all search attempts throughout the Bob Marshall Wilderness of northern Montana. Barry could only imagine the horror the Hanson family was feeling at this moment.

"Debbie, listen to me. I'm coming up to help. I'll leave right now. John and Merrilee Dawson can keep tabs on the ranch, so tell Grandpa Hanson not to worry. Do you hear me? We'll find Wendy. OK? She'll be all right. I'll be there in a few hours."

There was a long pause. Then Barry heard Debbie whisper a single word, a simple utterance that carried all the hope the frightened girl could muster. In a voice choked with dread she said "Hurry."

* * * * *

Ranger Perez studied the distant forms that sat by the campfire as he approached, his headlights illuminating the meadow with harsh brilliance.

Guiding his four-wheel-drive Trooper from the rugged path, he pulled into an open area by the tree line and switched off the ignition. Reaching down, he flipped another switch. This threw the area into darkness, save for the soft, flickering shadows tossed across the autumn grasses by the tiny flames.

He sat for a moment, listening to his engine ticking quietly as it cooled. How many times had this scene been repeated in his long career as a park ranger? How many anxious faces had looked up at him, waiting for word of missing family members and friends? It never got any easier. Never.

Now, sitting by the fire were two more people he must face. There was Tyler Hanson, a successful big-city lawyer who'd brought his family from the towers of Manhattan to the mountains of Montana in an attempt to escape a high-risk future filled with 70-hour work weeks and endless worldly attractions.

And next to him sat young Joey Dugan, the streetwise 17-year-old kid from East Village whose very life was being changed by the beauty and challenges of living on a working ranch.

How could he tell them that the chances of finding their missing family member were slim, especially after the sighting of the fallen horse? How could he ignore the past, the many searches that ended in heartbreak for everyone involved?

But his job description was clear. He was to care for the land, the animals, *and the people* who visited his wilderness, even if that meant turning his back on the obvious and hoping for the impossible.

"Evenin', gentlemen," he called as he lifted his camping gear from the back seat of the vehicle. "No rain tonight. That's good news for Wendy."

Mr. Hanson nodded. "Yeah," he said into the fire. "Rain wouldn't help matters."

Ranger Perez plopped his bundles down on the ground and knelt by the flickering flames to warm his hands. "Hi, Joey," he said with a smile. "Tyler has told me a lot about you over the last couple days. Says you're pretty good with a horse."

Joey smiled weakly.

The new arrival leaned back against a fallen log. "Hawk will be bringin' the rest of the family in by air at first light. My men will be arriving soon thereafter. We'll set up a base camp here in Parker's Meadow. You like that name? Thought it'd be fittin', since no one else knew it existed. Oh yeah, the doctor in Kalispell says the old codger's gonna pull through just fine. I think he's too pigheaded to die of a little thing like a bullet through the gut. Hospital said you did a fine job of patchin' him up, Joey. Boss Parker owes you his life."

"Wrangler Barry taught me," the boy stated.

"And speaking of Mr. Gordon," Ranger Perez continued, "he's on his way to Polson as we speak. He'll be flying in with the others tomorrow. I talked with Hawk on the radio. Said the whole Hanson clan is chafin' at the bit, ready to begin the search.

"Oh, and I've got a personal message for Joey from someone called Samantha." Joey looked up, a surprised smile lighting his young face. Ranger Perez slipped a small piece of paper from his coat pocket. "Didn't want to forget anything important so I wrote it down." He held the note toward the fire. "Says, 'Joey. You'll find Wendy OK. You found me once, didn't you?' "

The boy closed his eyes as warm tears moistened his cheeks. At his feet, flames crackled and popped, sending glowing sparks into the air where the gentle breeze carried them heavenward. High overhead they danced with the stars, then faded away.

* * * * *

Somewhere in the vast emptiness of space, a meteor slipped silently from the void and plunged into the earth's atmosphere, burning itself into oblivion. It left a thin line of light behind, creating a temporary crease in the canopy of night.

No one noticed its passing—not the trees or mountains, not even the river. The world was asleep, and except for a muffled roar coming from somewhere deep underground, there was no sound to disturb the silent night.

The stars looked down on a certain stretch of water as they had the night before, and the night before that. Rock outcroppings overhead had grown accustomed to the trembling bellow rising from somewhere unseen, deep inside the earth.

Calm waters reflecting the meteor's passing held the image for just a moment, then hurled it into a gaping hole where the ground shook and the river fell white with anger.

Suddenly there were only sounds; rasping, roaring echoes filled with deep-throated voices no one above could hear. The darkness became a living, breathing creature, prowling the under-earth, feeling its way along corridors untraveled by light.

Deeper, deeper, deeper the inky murkiness crept until even sound quieted itself, leaving the featureless world void of any element designed to disturb a human sense.

In this silent, visionless tomb, far from earth's surface, an unwelcome visitor lay still, unmoving, half buried in calm waters. Strands of short, blond hair moved in almost imperceptible cadence to some distant fluctuation of the shallow stream. A hand jutted from a sandy bank nearby, fingers curved, delicate, washed clean by the clear, cold liquid surrounding it. A booted foot rested atop a boulder, looking as if its owner had just kicked a field goal in some bizarre game, the leg's position frozen at the moment of uppermost swing.

The pale, seemingly lifeless face nestled between locks of matted hair gazed unseeing into the darkness, eyelids slightly ajar. Nose and mouth floated half submerged below the surface of the glassy stream, one nostril filled with sand and soil, the other sporting a thin trickle of red fluid. A tiny dried leaf drifted out of the open mouth, then paused. Slowly it moved back past the lips and disappeared, only to appear again. This was repeated over and over.

But there was no one to see this curious sight, deep in the bowels of the earth. High above, beyond the featureless walls of the subterranean chamber, past the distant roaring cataract and outcroppings of rock and twisted logs, only the stars looked down. And they remained as mute as death in the vast blanket of night.

CHAPTER 2

Day One—Morning

🐾 🐾 🐾

"Everyone gather 'round," Ranger Perez called as he spread a much-handled topographical map over a large boulder. The sun had been up for less than an hour and already the search parties had set up a base camp in the beautiful valley and eaten a daybreak breakfast prepared by Grandma Hanson and Lizzy Pierce.

Even before Hawk's floatplane appeared over the rim of the mountains and the all-terrain vehicles had found their way down the rugged trail, Mr. Hanson, Ranger Perez, and Joey had spent several hours planning the day's strategy by lantern light.

"Here's what we've got," the man announced as the group settled themselves in a semicircle about him. "Wendy Hanson is 11-year-old, stocky build, short blond hair. She was last seen wearing blue jeans, riding boots, and a brown leather jacket. A little over 24 hours ago she headed west, following the river out of this valley. Hawk has made a mark on my map where he thinks the waterway drops into a sinkhole of some sort. Wendy's horse was sighted at the mouth of the cavity. We presume the animal is dead."

Wrangler Barry reached over and drew Debbie close to him. "We can't know that for sure," he whispered. The girl nodded, biting her lip in an attempt to stifle a sob.

"Of course, we're hoping Wendy was thrown clear of the river when the horse fell. If that's the case, the girl would be on foot and couldn't possibly cover more area than I've marked with the yellow line.

"To make the most of our resources, I'm dividing us up into three search parties; Team A, Team B, and Team C."

The speaker bent over the map and pointed with a crooked stick. "Team A, made up of Ranger DeMitri and his men, will concentrate on the area north of the river from here to . . . here. I figure this is where she'll most likely be, so I'm putting my best trackers in this area. The terrain is mostly flat, so the four-wheel drive vehicles should make pretty good time checking things out.

"Team B, led by Barry Gordon, will keep south—"

"Ranger Perez," a hesitant male voice called from the gathering. "I . . . don't have a truck and I can't ride a horse. You see—"

The search director smiled. "That's no problem, Mr. Gordon. You take my Trooper. You and Debbie—"

"And me," came a distant disturbance. Everyone turned to see Samantha weaving toward the group under a shifting load of rope coils, a pickax, three canteens, a portable radio, and a box of crackers. "I'm going to find Wendy in five minutes, then we'll have a picnic and everyone's invited."

Ranger Perez grinned broadly. "And Samantha. Of course." Turning to Barry he continued. "I want you three to scout out the area south of the river. There's a narrow band of hikeable terrain running about five miles from this point to here. Wendy may have chosen to try that route in her effort to get out of the Bob Marshall. The search area is small, but so is Wendy. I don't want to leave any stone unturned."

Barry nodded, smiling over at the ranger. "Thank you," he said.

Mr. Perez winked, then looked again at the map. "I'll lead Team C. Tyler, Joey, and I will track the river on horseback to the sinkhole. Hopefully, we'll take the same route Wendy took, following any tracks she may have left behind. Lucky for us we had a small group of fresh horses waiting about four miles north of here, thanks to Joey's attempt to escort Boss Parker and young Peter Andrews out of the wilderness yesterday."

The group nodded approvingly in Joey's direction.

"And last but not least, our friend Hawk—Mr. Eye-in-the-Sky—will fly repeated missions over the entire area. We'll all be in radio contact with each other and with the elder Hansons and Lizzy Pierce at base camp. It's possible Wendy decided to retrace her steps and return to this valley. The base team will keep a sharp lookout, prepare meals, and fix sack lunches for the search parties, as well as keep in contact with outside authorities. They have the most powerful communications equipment. Grandpa Hanson will monitor all transmissions and bring in additional resources if we need them.

"Now," the ranger concluded, "after we do our jobs today, we'll either have found the little girl or have a pretty good idea where she's *not*. Understand?"

"We understand," came the collective reply.

"All right then, good hunting, everyone."

As the group began to break up, Grandpa Hanson lifted his hand. "I don't know how many of you are Christian," he called, "or believe in a Higher Power, but my family and I do. So does Wendy. If it's OK with everyone, I'd like to ask God to be with us in our search today."

Reverently, heads bowed and eyes closed tightly.

"Father in heaven," the old man began, his voice breaking slightly, "search by our side. Guide our minds and steps as we look for our little girl." His words faltered. After a long moment, he continued. "You know where she is. You know her condition. Reach down Your loving hand and hold her until we find her. Please, God. We ask this in Your Son's dear name. Amen."

"Amen," the group whispered.

* * * * *

Far from camp, at a place where the impossible happens, in the darkness of an unchartered chamber deep underground, a form stirred. The movement wasn't much. A passerby wouldn't have noticed. But the pale, delicately bent fingers of the hand jutting from the sand moved ever so slightly.

The tiny, dry leaf that had been floating in and out of the open mouth, drawn and expelled by the breath passing over it, suddenly flew away, driven by a crackling cough. Then all was quiet.

Wendy lay still, trying to fight the terrible sleepiness that pressed down on her like a weight. Was she in bed? Was she asleep under dark blankets piled high over her in the room she shared with Samantha at the Station? Is that why she couldn't see anything, couldn't move?

"Saman—" the word ground to a halt, choked by the sand and water half filling her mouth. She tried to spit, but found she could only roll the bitter mixture between her teeth and tongue.

Something was wrong. Something was terribly wrong! She wasn't home at the Station. She wasn't hiding under soft, warm blankets. She was cold, very cold. And there seemed to be water everywhere, even in her mouth.

Then she remembered. The river. Early stumbling. The rocks striking her shoulders and head.

There'd been a big, black hole in the ground; churning water rushing toward her—faster, faster—until everything went black—totally, completely black. Like now.

Wendy blinked. Then blinked again. A pain shot through her head like a searing knife driven into her scull. It caused her to cry out, the sound of her voice startling her as it echoed and reechoed, finally fading in some distant place.

But what place? Was she dead? No, she couldn't be. The first thing a dead person sees after waking up is Jesus, coming in bright, glowing clouds. Grandpa'd said so. Shown her a text in the Bible, and everything. This was nothing like that. Here was only darkness. Only cold and wet.

Using all her strength, she forced the gritty mixture of sand and water from her mouth. Then, laying her head back down, exhausted, she whispered the only thing she knew for sure. "I'm blind," she said.

* * * * *

Wrangler Berry guided the Trooper along the rock-strewn trail, shifting often as the ground rose and fell before him. "Getting kinda rough here," he called over the whine of the engine. "She wouldn't have covered many miles walking or riding on this side of the river."

Debbie nodded, her body swaying to the jerky movement of the vehicle. "Strange," she said.

"What's strange?" Barry wanted to know.

The girl thought for a moment. "This country seemed so beautiful a week ago. Now it's just scary, like a bad dream."

"I know what you mean," her companion sighed.

"Do you think we'll find her? I mean do you *really* think we will?"

Barry waited before he answered. "If it was anybody else out there wandering around the wilderness, I'd have my doubts. But Wendy's a different kind of animal all together. Remember when Red Stone rescued her from the mountainside? He had to set her broken leg and everything. But did that faze ol' Wendy? Not one bit.

"And last winter during the storm, who was it that swung from a rope halfway across the Dawsons' front yard to get wood out of a shed, which, as we all found out, she entered through the roof? Only Wendy would attempt such a stunt. But she did it. That girl always seems to get through whatever mess she's facing."

Barry paused. "I'm not saying surviving wandering around alone in the Bob Marshall Wilderness compares with her earlier escapades, but the same stubbornness and instinct that got her through before will certainly help her now, don't you think?"

"Unless the ground swallowed her up like it did the river," Debbie said, her voice unsteady.

"Now, don't be thinking such depressing thoughts," Barry pressed. "It won't help her or us. We've got to believe Wendy is trying as hard to be found as we are trying to find her. Right?"

Debbie nodded slowly. "It's not easy. Fear makes you think awful things."

Samantha's smiling face appeared between the driver and front-seat passenger. "Do you know what Lizzy told me?"

"What?" Barry asked, shifting gears.

"Lizzy said fear is like a shadow on the wall. It's not even real. You turn a light on, and *whoosh*, it runs away."

"And what does she mean by that?" Debbie asked.

The little dark-skinned girl shrugged. "I don't know. But whenever I'm in my room and I see something creeping on my wall like a monster or even a mountain lion, I turn on the light, and *whoosh*, it's history."

"Then what happens?" Wrangler Barry wanted to know.

"Then Wendy yells at me to turn off the light or she'll throw me out the window. But that's OK because I know if Wendy's awake, no monster or mountain lion has a chance in my room. I go right to sleep."

"I rest my case," Barry laughed, jabbing his thumb over his shoulder. "Monsters and lions aren't even a match for our Wendy. Maybe we should be feeling sorry for the Bob Marshall Wilderness, instead."

The Trooper bounced around a bend in the trail and continued on, leaving the pasture to the squirrels and chipmunks.

* * * * *

Hawk's Pacemaker rose on strong, outstretched wings, effortlessly gliding above the verdant landscape. The pilot scanned the ground, searching for any signs of a little girl with short blond hair and laughing eyes.

Under his left wing, the river coiled and twisted like an angry snake, slithering its way through innocent meadows and around forested hills.

He'd followed rivers before, many years ago in a faraway land where rice paddies and jungles carpeted the countryside. But on those flights, the wings carrying him through the hot, moist air were slung with weapons of war, deadly ordnance waiting to react with precision to his every command.

Above the drone of the Pacemaker, it seemed he could hear his radio crackling with the voices of men whose only goal was to destroy the enemy waiting below.

"Alpha Flight Leader to Tiger One. Alpha Flight Leader to Tiger One. Do you read? Over."

Hawk nodded. "I read five-by. This is Tiger One. Over."

"Fly heading zero three niner. Target fifteen northeast your position. Begin run at three thousand. Over."

"Roger that. Unloading 15 northeast from three."

"Smoke 'um good, Tiger One. No mercy."

"Roger. No mercy."

Hawk could feel his body press against the ejection seat of his Phantom F-4 fighter-bomber as he advanced the throttles. Lifting the aircraft's nose, he rolled inverted, then slowly moved the stick toward his belly, waiting until the line of trucks moving along the road below drifted through the targeting display projected on his windshield. With a gentle twitch of his right index finger, streams of tracers shot out before him, forming a temporary link to the dusty roadway.

He could see the vehicles skid to a stop as terror-filled occupants jumped out and dove for cover. His tracers walked the length of the convoy, igniting explosions as they passed through the metal skins of his targets.

A twist of his wrist brought the aircraft upright faster than a thought. With the burning convoy streaking toward him, he pressed yet another switch on the control yoke held securely in his gloved hand. He could hear the click, click-click of release bolts letting loose the bundles of bombs grouped below each wing. From the ground it looked as if the aircraft had tossed a collection of firewood earthward—the pieces falling end over end silently, coming closer and closer until they struck, enveloping the road, trucks, drivers, passengers, trees, and rice paddies in an instant inferno.

Somewhere above the roar of flames and muffled screams, the pop-pop of afterburners igniting could be heard. But on this road, on this hot, moist summer afternoon, there were no ears left to hear, nor eyes to see the jet streaking away to the horizon. The mission had been a success. As ordered, there had been no mercy.

Hawk's brow glistened in the cold cockpit of the Pacemaker as his mind shrank from the memory. "The people," he whispered. "The people are gone. They're all gone." A sob racked his sweating, trembling frame. How could he have done it—not once

DITD-2

33

but many times? How? And for what? Glory? Honor?

The Pacemaker droned on, slipping above the meadows and trees, obeying the commands of the crying man at the controls.

* * * * *

Joey reined in his horse and shook his head. "Tracks are leading to the bank again," he called, pointing. "Wendy must've crossed this river a dozen times. Why didn't she cut inland?"

"She figured the river would take her out of the wilderness," Ranger Perez stated, rubbing the back of his neck thoughtfully. "Seems our girl came up with a plan of action and was doing her best to stick with it. Can't fault her for that."

Mr. Hanson dismounted and knelt by the depressions in the sandy soil. "Early was well and happy at this point. See? The tracks are evenly spaced, with solid push-offs. Clippin' along at a pretty good pace, I'd say. No problems yet."

The lawyer's two companions nodded agreement. "Then we'd better keep at it," Ranger Perez encouraged. "With the other search teams flanking us on both sides of the river, we should find something, if there's something to find."

"There will be," Mr. Hanson said emphatically.

"Tyler," the ranger called softly. "There're no guarantees in the wilderness."

"I know that," the man snapped, then softened. "I appreciate the fact that you're trying to protect me from getting my hopes too high. But my little girl's out there. All I can do right now is ride this horse and do a lot of hoping. Until she's found I'm going to do *both* jobs as best I can."

"Understood," the ranger smiled.

Mr. Hanson hoisted himself into the saddle. Gathering up the reins, he turned the animal westward and clicked a gentle command. The three left the bank together, the roar of the river following them into the forest.

* * * * *

Wendy awoke with a start. She'd been dreaming of the Station, of her father and family, and of Early.

She lay still, listening to the void that pressed in on her from all sides. Only her breathing disturbed the dark silence.

"I'm a born loser," she stated aloud, hearing her words echo down unseen passageways. "I'm blind, and I'm scared of the dark."

The statement made her chuckle softly, causing the pain in her head to throb with each giggle. "Ouch!" she moaned. "No more jokes. Hurts to laugh."

She lifted her face above the water's surface and tried to look around, half expecting to see something. But all her eyes could perceive was total darkness.

Wendy pulled her hand and arm out from under their sandy blanket and tried to catch a glimpse of her fingers. Suddenly her palm bumped against her nose, causing her to jump.

"That was stupid," she said. "Scared by my own hand." Slowly she extended her arm and began feeling for what was around her. Her body to her waist seemed to be semisubmerged in shallow water while her legs and thighs were draped over a collection of rocks and piles of mud or sand.

She wiggled her toes, then flexed her knees. While each action produced some pain, it was tolerable.

She tested her elbows next, then her wrists and fingers. "Good," she sighed. "I'm all here. Now if I can just get everything to work together, I can do something really exciting like . . . sit up."

With a lot of huffing and puffing, straining and grimacing, she repositioned herself. "There," the girl announced, "I'm no longer lying in water. Now I'm sitting in mud. Personally, I consider that an improvement. Sure is cold here—wherever *here* is."

Wendy sat in silence for a long moment. "I really should figure out where I am, just in case someone wants to write." She spat out the remaining dirt and sand from her mouth while digging more from her nose. That's when she felt something sticky and crusty above her upper lip.

"Hold everything," she growled. "I thought I smelled dried blood. OK. Who's been bleeding around here? Come on, don't be shy." She wiggled her nose, wrinkled her forehead a couple times, then felt the skin below her hair line. There she discovered a deep gash a couple inches above her right eye.

"Medic!" she called, listening to her request echo in the distance.

A sudden shiver racked her aching frame. "OK, enough chit-chat. Time to figure out what's going on. The last thing I remember was taking a dip in Old Man River, then dropping into the ground through a big hole. Or was that a dream?" She turned her head from side to side. "I don't think it was a dream, 'cause this warm, cozy place sure isn't." She blinked. "Wait a minute! If me and the river were sucked into a giant hole, that means I'm *underground.* You know, like in a cave. A cave!"

For a moment Wendy sat listening to her own breathing. "I'm in a dark cave where no one can find me. *I* can't even find me. *And* I'm blind. Wait! Maybe I'm not blind. Maybe I'm just in a dark cave." She paused. "Or maybe there's all kinds of light bouncin' around and I just can't see it, which means I really *am* blind."

For the first time since waking, Wendy felt fear deep in the pit of her stomach. It rose slowly, like the fog drifting above Shadow Creek on cool autumn mornings. She suddenly realized the danger she was in. She'd left camp without telling anyone where she was going. Yes, she'd remembered to take provisions, but they were fastened to Early's saddle and he was probably miles away by now, eating meadow grass on some distant hilltop. For all practical purposes, she'd simply vanished, swallowed whole by the earth, doomed to spend her last days sitting sightless in a pile of cold mud, listening to herself die. Her breathing became erratic as fear took control. In the darkness she called out, but her word only returned to mock her. "Daddy . . . addy . . . addy . . . addy . . ."

* * * * *

Mr. Hanson reined in his horse as a sudden chill gripped his chest.

"What's the matter?" Joey called, stopping beside him.

"I . . . I don't know," the man said. "I just felt kinda strange."

Up ahead, Ranger Perez paused and waited for his companions. When they didn't continue in his direction, he cantered back toward them. "What's wrong?" he asked, studying the pair.

Mr. Hanson shook his head. "Forgive me. I . . . I just had this really scary feeling all of a sudden. Made my hands shake. See?" He held up gloved fingers. They were trembling. "Maybe I'm just hungry."

"Yeah, that's probably it," the team leader encouraged. "How 'bout we take a break and dig out some nourishment? My stomach's been grumbling for some time now." He glanced skyward. "It's almost noon. You fellas secure your horses while I check in with the other search parties." He moved to a nearby clearing and fished out his radio transmitter.

"Team Three to base. Team Three to base. Do you read?"

After a moment, he heard a strong, male voice respond. "Team Three, this is base. Hi, Ranger Perez. Did you find anything yet?"

"Hello, Grandpa Hanson," the speaker said, then paused. "Hope you don't mind if I call you that. Everyone else seems to."

He heard the voice on the line chuckle. "I'd be honored."

"Good. Now that we've got that settled, no, we haven't run into anything encouraging. Have the others checked in?"

"Barry called about 15 minutes ago, and I just heard from DeMitri. They're still looking."

Ranger Perez sighed deeply. "OK. I understand. How 'bout Hawk. Any word from him?"

"He went for gas about an hour ago. Should be back in the area any minute now."

As if on cue, the ground shook as the Pacemaker passed overhead at treetop level.

"I'll call you back, Grandpa Hanson," Ranger Perez radioed. "Hawk just rattled our molars."

"OK. Keep us informed. Base out."

The ranger twisted the frequency knob on his handset and held it to his ear. "Hey, Hawk. You 'bout knocked our heads off a second ago."

Hawk's voice crackled over the earpiece. "Is that you, Perez? I was just about to call you. Flew over the sinkhole on my way back from the lake. Strange thing. The horse is gone."

"What do you mean, the horse is gone?"

Mr. Hanson and Joey looked up sharply from their saddlebags.

"It's not there anymore. I flew three passes to make sure."

Ranger Perez pressed the handset closer to his ear. "Do you think it fell into the cavity?"

"Not really. Logs were still there, just like before. And I saw fresh tracks leading away from the lip, goin' south. Disappeared into the forest." There was a pause. "That silly critter's alive. I'm sure of it."

"Listen, Hawk," the ranger called, excitement lifting his words. "Get hold of Barry Gordon in my Trooper. Tell him to try to find the hole from his side of the river. I don't know if it's possible from where he's at, but it's worth a try. Maybe that animal can give us a clue to Wendy's whereabouts."

"Roger that," Hawk transmitted. "I'll give him a holler on his frequency. Catch ya later. Hawk out."

Ranger Perez frowned as he switched off his radio. "That's weird," he said, turning to his companions. "From the way you described him, I wrote that animal off as stone dead."

"I thought so, too," Mr. Hanson nodded. "Or at least injured seriously."

"Early's a tough critter," Joey added. "Just like Wendy."

The team leader nodded thoughtfully. "You know, I'm beginning to think that horse may have given us a pretty good clue as to where the girl is. See if you follow this. If anything had happened to Wendy prior to reaching the river, Early wouldn't have tried to cross those rapids by himself. Why should he? He would've headed inland."

Mr. Hanson's eyes narrowed as he nodded

slowly. "And the fact that we found the horse right by the river tells me that we should be concentrating our search along the shore. And not only that, we should zero in on the last mile before the sinkhole."

"Right," Joey agreed. "If Early had fallen into the rapids far upriver, he wouldn't have survived being carried by the currents. He's heavy, and those rocks would have pounded him to death." The boy began to shuffle his feet impatiently as thoughts clarified in his mind. "Since Early was able to untangle himself from those logs and bug out, he was just stunned, not dead. And *that* means he fell in not far from the hole. Since we know horses don't take chances when it comes to rushing water, Wendy had to be with him when he slipped."

Mr. Hanson's legs suddenly grew weak. He reached out and grabbed a tree limb for support. "Do you know what you're saying?" he gasped, face draining of color. "Our worst fears are coming true. I haven't been able to say this, but now I must. It's a good possibility that my little girl was tossed into the river just above the hole and . . . and . . ."

"And we'd better hurry if we want to find her before sundown," Ranger Perez encouraged, placing a gentle hand on the lawyer's shoulder. "Understand? We'd better concentrate all our efforts around the cavity. Early's shown us where to look."

"But the hole," Mr. Hanson breathed. "What if—"

"Let's not dwell on speculation just yet," the ranger warned. "We've got work to do. I'm going to tell everyone to change course and head for the area upriver of the sinkhole. We'll move base camp in as close as possible." The man unfolded his map and spread it across the ground. "Hawk can fly the Hansons, Lizzy Pierce, and our equipment to a calm stretch of river at the base of this mountain." He pointed with his finger. "We'll set up here, in this meadow. It's just three or four miles from the cavity. Any closer and he wouldn't be able to land. Water's too rough."

As Ranger Perez walked from the group to broadcast his new instructions, Joey looked over at his friend. "She didn't go in," he said. "She got caught on something, just like Early did. She's sittin' there tangled up on the bank waitin' for us to come get her—madder'n a hornet for taking so long. You'll see."

But Mr. Hanson wasn't listening. His ears were filled with the sounds of rushing water, and the imagined screams of his little girl.

Day One—Afternoon

Wendy reached out her hand hesitantly and felt the space surrounding her. The fear that gripped her heart raged a silent battle with a growing urge to survive in this cold, dark world.

Her fingers shook in terror at what they might find. Perhaps she wasn't alone in the black chamber. If the river had the power to carry her into the very bowels of the earth, other creatures could have fallen victim too—creatures unpleasant to meet on land, much less under it.

And what if the underground world contained unknown life forms, beings who roamed the sunless reaches of caves and caverns, feeding on victims tossed their way by heartless rivers?

"Steady," the girl whispered, addressing her vivid imagination as if it was a person sitting at her side. "Don't go makin' me crazy here. This isn't Star Trek."

Her hand brushed against something soft and moist. She instinctively withdrew her arm as if her fingers had touched fire. "Don't hurt me!" she pleaded. "I'm not all that tasty. Honest."

Nothing happened. No sound disturbed the awful silence.

She extended her arm again, this time letting her hand press against the mysterious object. It was firm underneath the soft covering. Pinching her fingers together, she pulled gently. Something broke off in her hand.

"Moss," she gasped. "It's a moss monster!"

The thought that a rock covered with this familiar plant had frightened her caused her to giggle. She liked the sound, so giggled again.

From somewhere far away, she heard another chuckle. Then another. "HEY!" she called.

"Hey!" came the reply. "YOU'RE MY ECHO!"

". . . my echo."

Wendy closed her eyes. "Knowledge," she whispered, so her echo wouldn't hear. "That's what Grandpa says chases fear away. I've got to get some knowledge goin' right away."

She pressed against the soft surface beside her. "That's a wall, a stone wall covered with wet moss. And the voice I hear talking to me is my own echo. RIGHT?"

". . . right?"

"Good, we all agree."

The girl sighed. "So, I'm in a cave sitting in the mud by a moss wall listening to myself talk. So far, so good."

Wendy could feel the terror that gripped her

44

heart begin to lose its hold.

"Now, there's the matter of whether I'm alone down here." She remained silent for a moment. "And, oh yes, I may be blind and really sitting in bright sunlight. But, no, that can't be happening because I don't feel any heat on my face."

She thought for a moment. "Then again, it might be night with no sun in the sky. I have no idea how long I've been here." Wendy sighed a frustrated sigh. "Boy, life sure can get complicated!"

Extending her arm above her head, she felt the air. "No roof. Must be a big room. I wonder if I can stand up."

Shakily, she maneuvered her legs until her booted feet were more or less under her. Then, with a lot of painful groaning, she managed to rise a few inches before slipping back into the mud.

She tried again, with the same results.

On the third attempt, she managed to stand, weaving back and forth drunkenly, feeling suddenly dizzy.

When she fell, she landed in a different spot, striking her head against something hard.

"OUCH!" she called, angered by her inability to remain on her feet. "This is hopeless," she groaned. "I can't even—"

The next word stuck in her throat as a new sound entered her dark world. It was soft, almost hidden under her own breathing. She pinched her nose and covered her mouth, lying absolutely still, listening, waiting. Yes, there it was again.

The sound was raspy, like a burst of air flowing through a long tube. She held her breath, feeling the fear she'd been fighting wash back over her. The awful truth struck hard. She was not alone.

* * * * *

Wrangler Barry stepped from the Trooper and painfully lowered himself to the ground. "It's Early, all right," he announced, running his fingers along the fresh imprints in the soft soil. "Joey and I put these shoes on her just before you guys came to the Bob Marshall Wilderness. Left front has a nick in it. See?"

Debbie nodded as she helped her friend stand. "He's limping, moving kinda slowly," Barry sighed. "I'd say Early's in trouble."

"What can we do?" the girl asked.

"Well, we've got to track him down first. He can't be too far ahead of us. Probably looking for open ground, meadow grasses to eat. But"—the wrangler stopped speaking while he adjusted his hat—"an injured animal can act strangely, you know, not normal. No tellin' what Early's plans are. The more severe the pain, the less rational will be his behavior. Same with people, I guess."

Debbie shivered. "Poor Early. All alone in this big wilderness."

"We may as well keep after him," Barry stated, starting back toward the Trooper. "I can't be much help on foot or horseback in the area everyone's heading now. We'll let them find the rider. Our team will concentrate on the horse. How's that sound to you?"

Debbie took hold of her companion's hand, stopping him. "Barry," she said, looking into his eyes. "You'd help find Wendy if you could. Everyone knows that."

The wrangler glanced away. "Doesn't make it any easier, Debbie. Wendy's lost and I can't do my part."

"But you are," the girl insisted. "You're trackin' Early. That's exactly what she'd want you to do."

Barry shook his head. "Look. All I know is, an 11-year-old girl is lost in the Bob Marshall Wilderness and I'm out huntin' a brown stallion with a chipped left front shoe. Doesn't exactly make me feel like a valuable part of the team."

Debbie stepped closer. "Well, what would you rather be doing?"

"I don't know!" The wrangler's face flushed with anger. "I don't know! These useless legs, this back; maybe huntin' horses is all I'm good for. How can I face Wendy when this is all said and done? 'Hey, Barry? What did you do to help save me?' 'Oh, I rode around in a car looking for your horse.' "

"You're not being fair to yourself," Debbie countered.

"Fair? *Fair*?" Barry moved toward the girl in an almost threatening manner. Debbie didn't budge. "Oh, I stopped worrying about what's fair and what isn't last spring. Sure, I accept my injuries. I accept the fact that every one of my dreams got blown

47

away in that blizzard. But don't expect me to sit back and say, That's OK, life can be a bowl of cherries even though you can't ride a horse or help save a little girl's life. It's not that easy, Debbie. The hurt has spread from my legs to my heart. I can't get rid of it. I don't know what I'm good for. I don't know what to think when I look in the mirror. Am I Barry the horseman? Am I Barry the invalid? What am I? You tell me, Debbie. What am I good for?"

The girl gazed into the eyes of her companion without speaking. His question frightened her. She'd fallen in love with an energetic, hardworking wrangler who loved life and lived to break and ride powerful horses. Now, the man leaning on a cane in front of her was someone who in many ways had become a stranger. Gone was the fiery zest for living. Gone were the dreams he'd shared with her during long summer evenings by the footbridge. What *was* left for them? How could she hope to follow him into the future when there seemed to be no place to go?

"I don't know, Barry," she said softly. "I don't know how to answer you."

The wrangler's look turned from anger to anguish. "I'm scared, Debbie. I'm scared about tomorrow, and the next day, and the next. People tell you that love will see you through anything. Well I love you and I think you love me, but it isn't enough. Maybe we both need to realize that fact."

The girl fought back a sudden sob. "I'm not ready to," she said. "I'm just not ready to."

Barry closed his eyes and leaned forward as

Debbie pressed her flushed cheek against his, gently wrapping her arms around the man's sagging shoulders. "Don't give up," she whispered. "Oh, please, Barry. Don't give up on us."

The two stood for a long moment as the noonday sun shone through the canopy of branches. Far in the distance, the drone of Hawk's Pacemaker filled the valleys and hills as the tiny aircraft dipped below the mountaintops and began dropping toward an unseen river.

* * * * *

"Is there enough room to land?" Grandpa Hanson called to the pilot as he watched the tiny stretch of calm water race in their direction.

"Sure," Hawk acknowledged, his eyes not leaving the approaching river. "Water'll slow us quickly, once we touch down. The trick is to plant the floats as soon as possible, leaving what's left of the landing area for stopping. This ain't exactly Kennedy Airport, but we're not exactly a jumbo jet. It'll be tight, so everybody hold on."

Grandpa Hanson glanced at the backseat passengers and smiled weakly. His wife and Lizzy sat surrounded by tent stakes, food supplies, sleeping bags, and a colorful assortment of camping gear. "How you doin' back there?" he called.

Lizzy nodded. "Can't say much about the meals in this airliner, but," she pointed out the side window, "the movie's topnotch."

Grandma Hanson grinned. "Just hope they don't

lose any of our luggage."

Hawk reached up and retarded the throttle, lessening the roar of the big radial engine thundering just beyond the firewall. "Please return your tray tables and seatbacks to their upright and locked positions," he announced with enthusiasm, using his best airline-pilot voice. "We'll be landing sooner'n a groundhog dives for cover."

Grandpa Hanson was about to respond when, BUMP, the Pacemaker hit the surface of the river, blasting white spray from under the shuddering floats. The pilot and passengers felt the firm grip of the water as the aircraft quickly slowed and came to rest, rocking gently in its own wake.

"Piece of cake," Hawk called, pointing his noisy conveyance in the direction of the nearby riverbank. "Had room to spare."

"Where?" Grandpa Hanson gasped, studying the row of half-submerged logs they would have collided with had they gone 30 feet farther.

Hawk grinned and brought the Pacemaker to a grinding halt on the shore. "Welcome to the new base camp airport, serving residents of the high meadows and all lost little girls in need of saving. We hope you enjoyed the trip. Your luggage will either be on this aircraft or on its way to Istanbul. Have a nice day."

Grandma Hanson chuckled as she unfastened her seat belt and pushed open the cabin door. "I think I'm sitting on lunch," she laughed.

"Mashed potatoes again?" her husband teased.

Lizzy chuckled, trying her best to move her legs. "I've never worn a tent before," she called.

Hawk shook his head. "Sorry 'bout the tight fit, ladies. But it'll save us a trip. I'll head back now to get the remainder of our gear. Should return in under 30 minutes. What takes hours by horseback is only a short hop in my old feathered friend." He patted the top of the instrument panel lovingly.

Grandpa Hanson grinned. "Anything to help us find Wendy is a welcome addition to the team, even if it smells like oil and old fabric. We're glad you're here."

After a few minutes spent off-loading the camping gear, Hawk hurried back into the aircraft and settled himself in the pilot's seat. Grandpa Hanson reached up to close the cabin door when Hawk spoke. "Grandpa Hanson, may I ask you something?"

"Sure," the old man said smiling, resting his arms on the back seat.

Hawk sighed deeply and looked up at the blue sky. "This God of yours, the One you prayed to this morning, what's He like?"

Grandpa Hanson chuckled. "First, He's not *my* God, He's *our* God—yours, mine, everybody's. And if I had to describe Him to someone who doesn't know Him yet, I'd say He was kind, forgiving, interested in our lives."

"What if . . ." the pilot paused. "What if our lives haven't always been like . . . like we wanted them to be? You know? What if we did some things that we didn't know was wrong until later? Does God hate us for that?"

The Pacemaker's wings rocked gently in the cool breezes as Grandpa Hanson formed an answer to Hawk's question. "Our heavenly Father isn't so concerned about the past," the old man said quietly. "He likes to focus on the present, on what we're doing right now."

"But," Hawk pressed, "isn't God like a judge? Doesn't He make us suffer for our sins? That's what the preacher was always tellin' us when I was a little kid. I can hear him now. 'Do wrong and you'll burn in hell.'" The man looked down at his workworn hands resting on the control stick. "Isn't that the way it is?"

Grandpa Hanson smiled a gentle smile. "I think we need to talk about this," he said. "There are things about the Almighty you need to know. You might be surprised at what Jesus had to say about His Father."

"Jesus? What's He got to do with it?"

The old man swung the Pacemaker's door around in preparation for closing it. "Everything," he said. "He has everything to do with it. You gotta know Jesus before you can understand God the Father. We'll talk more about it tonight. OK?"

Hawk smiled. "OK. Tonight."

The Pacemaker's props clicked around a couple times before spinning to life amid a blue cloud of smoke and a deep-throated roar. As he taxied out onto the river, his mind played Grandpa Hanson's words over and over again. "You gotta know Jesus before you can understand God the Father."

Strange. The old man hadn't seemed concerned when he'd told him there might be some problems in his past. What was it about Jesus that made the difference? Won't all sinners burn in hell? Doesn't God put them there? The Pacemaker swung into the wind. Had that friendly, Bible-thumping pastor who shouted and waved his arms from the pulpit each week been wrong?

With these thoughts tumbling about in his mind, Hawk pushed the throttle forward and felt the Pacemaker begin its take-off run. He caught a glimpse of his three ex-passengers waving from the riverbank as he roared by. A tiny spark of hope flickered in the pilot's heart. Would he finally find a way to accept his past and still believe God loved him?

In the vibrating cockpit of the old airplane climbing higher and higher above the landscape, another search had begun.

* * * * *

Wendy hadn't heard the sound for a long time now. She'd sat as silently as she could, listening to the ringing in her ears. Whoever, or *what*ever, had been in the dark chamber with her must have gone, silently slipping away while she waited wrapped in terror.

A tear tumbled from the corner of her eye and splashed into the water, leaving behind a tiny *plurp* to announce its fall. The girl had never felt so alone, so cut off from the world she believed was now, and forever, out of reach.

I must be dying, she thought to herself. *This must be the way it feels to die. First there's some pain, and then your heart begins to beat faster and faster, like mine is doing right now. But I don't want to die. I don't want to. I want to live on Shadow Creek Ranch with Debbie and Daddy and Grandma and Grandpa and Lizzy and Joey and Samantha.* Another tear fell unseen from her cheek. *But they can't find me. They'll never find me. No one knows where I am. No one.*

Wendy began to cry in a way she hadn't cried for a very long time. It was the weeping of a tiny child, almost infantlike. In the darkness, she drew her legs up against her chest and folded her arms about them.

Scenes from her life moved through her mind like a motion picture played slowly. There was her mother's face, that pretty smile, loving eyes. And Daddy, holding her close when he'd come in late from work and she was already asleep in her room with the animals printed on the wallpaper.

The girl smiled in the darkness as the visions continued. There was Debbie, tall and perfect, sitting across from her at the breakfast table, eating buttered toast and talking about something important. Debbie's laugh always made her happy.

Next, images of the ranch. Of Early. Joey fussing at her, the anger in his words never showing in his eyes. And little Samantha gathering wildflowers in the pasture while Grandpa and Grandma walked hand-in-hand nearby. Such wonderful images! Such peaceful pictures!

She saw a night sky littered with stars and Dad's voice talking low. What was he saying? Yes. She heard it. He was speaking about the Power that put the stars in the heavens. He'd pointed and said, "Look beyond the mountains, Wendy, beyond the clouds and stars. That's where God lives. But don't think you can hide from His loving eyes. He sees you, Wendy, and cares about you. He always will."

The girl's breathing slowed as the images faded. From her lips came a quiet plea; a question heard by no human ear. "God?" she asked. "Can You see me now?"

* * * * *

Mr. Hanson came upon it first, then Joey and Ranger Perez. The three edged toward the lip of the cavity cautiously, listening to the thunderous roar and feeling the ground shake under their boots. No one spoke as they tried to take in the awesome sight.

To this point, there'd been no human tracks leading away from the river. Only the telltale signs of a horse slipping on the bank 100 yards back. The three searchers had looked in vain for even the slightest indication that Wendy had fallen off Early before the animal tumbled into the rushing waters. But no boot prints, no broken branches, no pieces of cloth, not one shred of evidence offered itself up to their painstaking scrutiny.

Hours of searching had brought them here, to

the very edge of the impossible. Mr. DeMitri and his team had seen nothing north of the river. Wrangler Barry's party was now tracking Early to the south. They hadn't stumbled on any sign of the missing girl, either.

Mr. Hanson held tightly to a low branch and peered into the gaping, dark gash in the ground. The cavity seemed to be drawing the very air into its open mouth as it drank the river without swallowing.

"Man!" Joey called. "I thought it looked big from the air. But standing next to it, it's huge! This is the most bizarre thing I've ever seen, and that's saying a lot, seeing as I'm from East Village."

Ranger Perez eyed the depression thoughtfully. "What do you think? A hundred? Hundred and fifty feet across?"

"I'd say close to 150," Mr. Hanson shouted, backing away cautiously. "Can't tell how deep. Just dark shadows and a lot of boiling, rising mist down there." He shook his head. "Not a very pleasant place. Let's concentrate our search upriver a little more. We've got an hour of daylight left. Maybe we'll find—"

"Tyler," Ranger Perez interrupted, trying to be heard above the roar. "She's not upriver. We looked."

"Well," the younger man shrugged. "Maybe we missed something. Maybe—"

"Wendy was on the horse when it fell," the ranger pressed gently. "Maybe it's time you admitted that to yourself."

"NO!" Mr. Hanson cried out, lifting his hands in a pleading gesture. "No. She got off somewhere. Early went in alone."

"But, Tyler—"

"Don't tell me my little girl fell into this hole!" The lawyer's face reddened. "Don't tell me that! She's in the forest somewhere, waiting for us right now."

Ranger Perez stepped forward. "Tyler, you must—"

"NO ONE SAW IT HAPPEN! DO YOU HEAR ME? WE CAN'T KNOW FOR SURE!" The man fought back angry sobs. "We can't know for sure. I won't believe it until someone looks me in the eye and says they saw Wendy drop into this . . . this . . . place. So, we go upriver and look again. Do you hear me? We search upriver!"

Ranger Perez stood for a long moment, studying the anguished face of his companion. He knew the man's heart was breaking. He knew the terrible fear his friend was feeling at this very moment; a fear unutterable. Mr. Hanson wasn't allowing himself to believe what all the signs were indicating. As head ranger in a wilderness back country, he'd seen it before. The experience never got any easier to take.

"OK," the leader agreed softly. "We'll backtrack 'til dusk, then head for base camp. You're right, Tyler. We may have missed something. Let's take another look."

The lawyer nodded enthusiastically and moved

away from the cavity, half running in the direction of the tethered horses. Joey watched him with growing uneasiness. What was going on? Why were they heading upriver? If Wendy had, in fact, dropped into this gaping hole in the Montana mountains, they should concentrate their efforts right here, shouldn't they?

"Ranger Perez," the boy called. "I don't think she's back there."

"I know," the man said.

"Then . . . why are we . . ."

Mr. Perez pointed at their companion. "He wants proof."

"Of what?"

"That he may have lost his little girl forever."

Joey's heart skipped a beat as the ranger's words sank in. During all their hours of searching, he'd never believed that Wendy was dead, only lost. Even if the girl had been carried into the hole, she was down there waiting for them, wasn't she?

He turned and gazed into the angry darkness just beyond the stony lip of the cavity. It couldn't be true. Not Wendy. Not that silly little girl who seemed to enjoy bugging him all the time, trying to make his life miserable with her stubborn ways and off-the-wall ideas. No. Wendy wasn't dead. She couldn't be.

Joey turned and faced the ranger. "I don't know what to do," he said, his voice choked.

Ranger Perez nodded and glanced at Mr. Hanson. The man was sitting astride his horse, waiting by the edge of the forest. "Neither does he," the ranger sighed.

* * * * *

Barry Gordon leaned heavily on his cane and gazed into the lengthening shadows. Going had been slow for most of the afternoon. Early's tracks had led them from meadow to woods, streambed to rocky knoll, but not once had they caught even the most tentative glimpse of their illusive quarry.

"One thing's for sure," he called over his shoulder at the others waiting in the Trooper. "Early's gettin' weaker. From what I can tell, he hasn't even stopped to eat. Just wanders about like a drunk staggering down Babcock Street. That horse really got shook up by his dip in the river."

Debbie zipped her coat all the way up to her neck, trying to ward off the dropping temperature. "Maybe we'd better head back to base camp before it gets any darker. I could use a warm fire and some hot soup. We can pick up our search right here tomorrow. Whadda ya say?"

Barry nodded. "You're right. Not much light left." The man turned and hobbled back to the vehicle. "Sure thought we'd catch up with him by now. If I was on horseback, I could've." He slid into the driver's seat and pulled his lap belt and shoulder harness across his legs and chest. "Trooper's too slow in this country. Besides, horses are better for trackin'."

Debbie placed her hand on his. "We'll find him tomorrow," she said.

Samantha, who sat bundled in blankets on the back seat, reached up and patted Barry on the neck. "We all can't fit on a horse," she laughed. "I'd keep falling off the rear end and land in a mud puddle and you'd have to stop and wash me off and get me back up. Then I'd fall off again. Trooper's much cleaner. See? I'm not even muddy."

Debbie smiled at their diminutive team member. "And we're very glad you're not."

Barry spun the wheel and shifted into first gear. "Everything's better on horseback," he said softly.

Debbie leaned her head against the tall seat and watched the darkening shadows bump by beyond the window glass. Maybe tomorrow would bring some good news for a change. Maybe, with the morning light, someone would find a lead, a piece of evidence, anything to show the search teams where Wendy and her wayward horse were hiding.

She looked over at the driver and studied him for a long moment. And perhaps in the night hours, she'd be able to formulate a plan to help her hurting friend deal with the unfortunate turns his life had taken during the past year.

With a whine the sturdy, green vehicle crested a hill and disappeared into the shadows.

* * * * *

"Look at that!" Joey blinked a couple times to make sure he was seeing what he was seeing. Was the gathering darkness playing tricks on his tired eyes, or was that a cabin hidden between the rocks?

60

Finding such a structure in the Montana wilderness wasn't unusual. But discovering one jammed into a rocky outcropping 30 feet above a roaring river certainly deserved a second look. Ranger Perez and Mr. Hanson sat up in their saddles, mouths dropping open in surprise. "Well, lock me up and bury the key," the team leader gasped. "If I didn't know any better, I'd say that's the old Stanfield place. But what in blue blazes is it doing three miles from where Justin Stanfield built it?"

"Maybe a better question would be, What's a cabin doing hanging out in space above a roaring river?" the lawyer stated.

The riders gazed wordlessly at the mysterious sight, feeling the cold winds of night beginning to rise about them. The sun, and its warmth, had slipped behind distant mountains half an hour back, throwing the wilderness into a state of cold, dim shock. Only enough light remained to recognize shapes and forms, even if one of those happened to be a splintered but still structurally sound cabin jutting from an outcropping high overhead.

"We missed it the first time," Joey said. "Guess we were too intent on the tracks by the riverbank. And we didn't see it from the air, either. Musta been hidin' behind those trees."

Ranger Perez scratched his head. "How can a cabin, which used to be somewhere else, end up perched above a river lookin' like an oversized eagle's nest? This is weird."

"Not as weird as the fact that there's someone

still living in it," Mr. Hanson called from nearby where'd he'd moved for a better look.

Joey and Ranger Perez hurried to their companion's side and let out a collective gasp. In the section of the cabin wedged between two boulders, they discovered a light, a faint light, casting an erie glow from a broken window and illuminating the cold stone face of the cliff.

"Now I've seen everything," Joey said, shaking his head.

Ranger Perez adjusted his hat and rubbed a sore spot on his arm. "I think we'd better investigate," he announced with authority. "Maybe whoever's up there saw what happened yesterday. Wouldn't hurt to check it out."

Mr. Hanson nodded. "If someone is crazy enough to live in a cabin that's stuck out over a rushing river, I don't know if I'd trust his, or her, judgment."

The ranger shrugged. "It's all we've got for now. Let's pay our wilderness neighbor a visit before he goes to bed—or falls into the river, whichever comes first."

Joey chuckled. "This is gonna be interesting."

The three secured their horses at the edge of the forest and moved quickly upriver, searching for a spot to cross the angry currents. Once on the other side, they scrambled up the steep embankment, using whatever finger- and toeholds they could find.

By the time the searchers had reached a spot just above the cabin, night had completely wrapped the Bob Marshall Wilderness in its dark grip. To the east, above distant mountaintops, a full moon was rising, buffing the land to a silver luster and sending dark shadows deep into the surrounding woodlands.

A well-worn path led them the last 20 feet to the front door. Three-quarters of the cabin rested on a semiflat slab of rock while the other quarter hung, splintered and broken, out into space. The little building had arrived at its present location rather violently, as evidenced by the cracked roofline and the shattered wall pressed against the granite face of the escarpment.

The three gathered by the bent frame of the front door. "Should I knock?" Ranger Perez whispered.

Mr. Hanson wrinkled his brow slightly. "What do you usually do when you visit someone in the wilderness?"

"Well, most cabins are flat on the ground, not hanging out in midair."

"Knock," Joey urged, edging away from the dark precipice, "but not too hard."

Ranger Perez cleared his throat and tapped lightly on the door jam.

At that instant, the portal burst open, almost sending the three visitors hurling off the cliff. "Who's there?" a voice called loudly. "I know someone is there! I heard you talking. No, you weren't talking. You were whispering. I don't like whispering. Makes me nervous. If you have something to say, just come out and say it."

"Are you Justin Stanfield?" the team leader

asked, trying to regain his composure and balance.

"Who's askin'?"

"I'm Ranger Perez, from the Spotted Bear Station."

The three saw a form silhouetted against the light spilling from inside the cabin. "Perez? Perez? Oh, yes. I know who you are. You're not dangerous."

"No, I'm not," the visitor replied, moving toward the door. "What are you doing here?"

"Who are these people with you?" came the quick reply.

"Tyler Hanson and Joey Dugan. They're from near Bozeman."

Joey squinted, trying to make out the features of the man standing in the doorway. "What happened to your cabin?" he asked timidly.

"You talk funny," the shadowed figure stated.

Mr. Hanson extended his hand. "He's from New York City. So am I. We moved to Montana a couple years ago."

"What're you doin' here in the wilderness?"

Ranger Perez smiled and motioned toward the door. "May we come in?"

"Why?"

The man shrugged. "Because it's cold out here and I don't want to fall into the river."

"I should hope not," the dark form responded. "River's mean. Doesn't like people. Hates 'em. I should know. Tried to take me once, but I out-smarted it."

"So, may we come in?"

"Oh, I suppose. But don't track up the place. I try to keep things tidy."

The figure moved away from the door, allowing the light cast by a single oil lamp to illuminate his face for the first time. He was young, probably around 30 years old. He sported an unkempt tangle of surprisingly snow-white hair. His face reminded Joey of a picture he'd once seen of the scientist Albert Einstein.

Justin Stanfield was also short in stature. He wore a red sweater smudged with ash, and a pair of threadbare, cotton pants that ended about five inches shy of his bony ankles. Leather sandals covered his feet and in his left hand he held what looked like a long, slender paintbrush.

"You can't stay long," the man announced, suddenly hurrying away as if remembering something. "Got work to do. Don't like visitors when I'm creating. Makes me nervous."

The three entered the cabin and were greeted by a warm, potbelly stove and the smell of baking bread. The front room was small, with a table and a few chairs scattered randomly about. A cot, burdened with a pile of blankets and a thin pillow, rested comfortably against the far wall. The room had two doors. One hung open, the other was closed.

But the most notable feature of the room were the walls. They were covered with colorful oil paintings, each delicately depicting a scene from nature. Some held wild animals within their carefully fashioned wooden frames, others presented in subtle hues and bold lines images of the land, introducing each mountain and valley with grace and reverence.

"Don't touch anything!" came the disembodied command through the open door. "Paint could be wet. Takes time for oil-based dyes to dry. You start poking around and next thing you know, I've got finger prints all over my skies. I hate when that happens. Have to repaint the clouds and everything. You want any food?"

Ranger Perez leaned forward and studied the detailed depiction of a mountain lion sunning itself on a rock. "Something smells delicious."

"It's bread. Made it myself. Can't exactly order out around here."

Joey chuckled. "You paint good," he said.

"What do *you* know about art? You're from New York."

The boy frowned. "Hey, I know culture. I used to do a little painting myself, 'cept I didn't use no fancy brushes or expensive canvases. I was more into spray cans and brick walls."

"I may have seen your work," Mr. Hanson laughed.

Joey smiled. "Even did a custom job on the police chief's squad car. He wasn't exactly pleased, although, if you ask me, that ol' Ford of his looked pretty good when I was done."

"No, no, no," the cabin's resident countered, reentering the front room, wiping his hands on a damp cloth. "Art isn't supposed to make something look good. It should re-create it, make it new, complete, fresh."

"Well, the police chief didn't use those words to describe my work," Joey said with a grin.

"I'll bet," Mr. Hanson chuckled.

Ranger Perez stepped forward. "So, Justin, are you going to tell us how your cabin got here?"

"The river," the artist said, lowering his voice as if afraid someone would overhear. "It does what it wants to do. Know what I mean?"

"The river moved your cabin?"

"You think *I* put it up here?" Justin gasped, shaking his head. "Hey, I like nice views as much as the next guy, but I'd choose a less—how shall I say—*precarious* plot of land. Maybe a spot with a lower elevation."

"How did it happen?"

The man swung open the iron door of his stove and tossed in a handful of small logs. "Well, I go out to do some painting, you know, the usual stuff I do. It rains some that day but I think, no big deal. Rains a lot this time of year.

"I come home that evening and, instead of a yard, vegetable garden, and cabin in my clearing, there's this river flowing by like it's been there since Creation. I swear I'm tellin' you the truth. Everything was gone. So I spend the night in the forest and at first light start hunting for my missing house. I follow this fool out-of-nowhere waterway for about three miles and bingo, there sits my cabin up in these rocks. Don't ask me how it landed here. I figured the water got dammed up somehow, then the bottom fell out, literally. The river began dumping itself into that big hole in the ground. Left my little abode hanging up here like a monkey in a tree. What am I supposed to do? Leave? This cabin is all I've got. So, I move back in.

"The place was an absolute mess but, luckily, nothing important was busted, 'cept my guest room. It kinda doesn't have a floor anymore."

"You have guests?" Mr. Hanson questioned.

"Yeah, but they don't stay long."

The three visitors blinked and looked at each other.

"It's a joke!" Justin laughed. "You're the first visitors I've had since my . . . relocation." The man withdrew a pan filled with brown, freshly baked wheat rolls from the stove. "Hungry?" he asked.

Mr. Hanson stepped forward. "Where were you yesterday?"

The artist looked up surprised. "You a cop?"

"No. Were you here in your cabin?"

"Maybe I was and maybe I wasn't."

Ranger Perez lifted his hand. "Hold on, guys. We're gettin' off on the wrong foot. Justin. We're searching for a little girl, 11 years old, who wandered off alone, following this river."

The man laughed then suddenly sobered. "You shouldn't try to follow this river," he said, leaning forward. "That would be a mistake. Bad things might happen."

"Yes, we know," the ranger agreed. "But, nonetheless, this girl—her name's Wendy—tried to leave the Bob Marshall using this route. We're looking for her. This is her father."

"I didn't see any girl." Justin announced, becoming agitated. "You've got to go now. Got paintings to finish. My new meadow scene needs a framing tree and—"

"Are you sure you didn't see anything?" Ranger Perez urged.

"Look. I'm an artist. I observe the world differently than most folks. Sometimes I see things and I don't know if they're real or just my imagination." The man hurried to the window and peered into the darkness, his back to his guests. "People say I'm crazy. They say I cooked my brain on drugs when I was younger. Maybe they're right. I'm not exactly proud of my past. But one thing's for sure. I see stuff others don't see. That's why I paint. I create images in my mind and then put them on canvas." He turned. "Are you sure you won't have some biscuits? Might even have a jar of preserves in the cupboard."

Mr. Hanson moved in his direction, hand outstretched, palm down. "She's about this high. Has blond hair and blue eyes. Stocky build."

The artist backed away. "I didn't see anything." His face paled and his eyes started blinking rapidly. "Honest. There's been no girl and horse by here in days."

"Horse?" Joey said stiffening. "We didn't say nothin' about a horse."

By now the artist's hands were trembling. "Look. I'm kinda messed up. You know? The things

I see could just be my imagination playing tricks on me. You can't trust what I say. Just last month I saw the river move. That's right. It turned upstream and everything dried up like a desert. Then a few days later it was back like it never left. That's crazy. I'm crazy. You gotta believe me."

"Did you see my little girl?" Mr. Hanson pressed, his voice rising. "She came by here. Her horse was spotted in the woodpile at the lip of the hole."

"There's no horse down there!" Justin shouted, pointing out the dark window. "Go look for yourself. It's not there."

"We know," the lawyer said. "It's gone."

"There! That proves it. You can't believe what you see by the river. Even you admit that first there's a horse, then there isn't. The river does that. It makes you believe what isn't true."

"I think you saw Wendy," Mr. Hanson announced coldly, moving even closer. "I think you saw her by the river yesterday. Tell me what happened. Tell me right now!"

"Easy, Tyler," Ranger Perez warned, placing his hand on his companion's shoulder.

"He knows," the lawyer said without turning, his eyes fastened on the frightened man. "He saw what happened."

"NO!" the artist cried. "It was just my imagination playing tricks on me. Sometimes it does that, you know? It's the drugs I took when I was younger. You gotta believe me. I didn't see your little girl fall off her horse. I didn't see the river reach up and

grab her and drag her down into its cold heart."
Sweat and tears moistened the man's flushed face.
"You've got to believe me! I didn't see her strug-
gling, hitting those rocks so hard, gasping for air."

Justin fell back against the table, sending cups
and dishes clattering to the floor, his eyes filled
with terror. "And I didn't see that sweet little girl,
that precious child, go into the hole with the river.
No. It didn't happen! I imagined it all. You gotta believe me. Please. Believe me!"

Mr. Hanson stood unmoving, staring at the
artist. No one spoke. The only sound disturbing the
silence was the roar of the river below, and the muffled growl of tons of water being sucked unseen into
the black earth.

CHAPTER 4

Day Two—Morning

🐾 🐾 🐾

Wendy stirred, letting out a low moan as consciousness fought its way through her numb mind and aching body. She was cold, colder than she'd ever been in her life. It seemed that she was no longer a human being lying in mud, but rather, through some transformation she didn't understand, she'd *become* mud. Wendy Hanson didn't exist anymore. Now she was part of the darkness, part of the soil. In the hours since she'd been taken, she and her surroundings had joined. No longer was she a captive of the river. She *was* the river.

"I belong here," the girl whispered, her lips moving almost imperceptibly as she spoke. "This is my world. Up there, in the light, I'm a stranger."

She paused, listening to her heart beat. It sounded weak, indifferent, lonely. She could feel water pressing against her skin like a cold blanket. It was all around her, under her, covering her legs and stomach.

"You win," she said, the words more a movement

of her tongue than an utterance. "You win, river. You've swallowed me up and taken away the light. I can't fight you anymore."

Something was hurting, but Wendy wasn't sure exactly where. Was it her right knee? Her arm? No, it was her knee. At least, she thought so. The girl shifted her weight slightly. "Ouch!" she cried, the word sounding rough in her ears. Yes, there was definitely something sharp sticking into her right kneecap.

"Wait a minute," Wendy said, lifting her head a little, trying to clear her throat. "Rivers don't hurt. They don't have feelings. But people do." Her mind swirled in confusion as she tried to make sense of thoughts drifting without anchor about her head. "Rocks and trees and bushes don't hurt. They don't speak or think. But I do. I feel pain. I feel fear. What does that mean?"

"What do you think it means?" a voice called from nearby.

Wendy jumped at the sound. "Who's there?"

"Me, silly," came the answer.

"You . . . you sound just like me."

"Well, of course I do. I *am* you, at least the you you used to be."

Wendy tried to peer into the inky blackness but gave up, closing her eyes with a deep sigh.

"You can't see me," the voice called. "I'm invisible. Remember? Isn't that what you told Joey when he didn't want you to go on the camping trip with trail boss Parker and you said you could be invisible?"

73

"But I . . ."

"Well, isn't that what you said?"

The girl paused, then spoke softly. "Yes."

"That was a stupid thing to say. You're not invisible because you exist. And if you exist, people can see you. Get it?"

Wendy groaned. "Why are you talking to me like this?"

"Because someone has to. Someone's got to talk some sense into that thick skull of yours. I mean, look at you. You're lying in cold mud, blind as a bat. No one knows where you are, you haven't eaten for who knows how long, and you're ready to give up. You make me sick!"

The girl coughed softly. "I don't want to die," she said. "But I don't know how to live, anymore."

"There, you see?" the voice mocked. "What kind of harebrained thinking is that? Of course, you don't want to die. Only idiots *want* to die. But living is harder than dying. I figured that out a long time ago. As a matter of fact, the terrible truth is that life hurts."

"So?"

The voice laughed in the darkness. "So as long as you are hurting, you know you're alive and can do something smart to get out of the mud. Sometimes you can be so ignorant!"

Wendy began to cry. "Don't talk to me like that. I'm scared. I don't know what's going to happen next."

The voice sighed audibly. "Haven't you been listening? Haven't you heard a word I've said? Hurting proves you're alive. And if you're alive, which you are, you can do something to stop the hurt."

"What? Do what?"

"THINK!" The word seemed to echo up and down unseen passageways. "Are you listening to me? When everything seems impossible, don't freak out. Just stop and think."

"I . . . I can't."

"Yes, you can."

Wendy lay still for a long moment, her breathing suddenly coming in short, heavy gasps. "Will you stay with me?" she called out.

There was no response. Only silence.

The voice had been right. Wendy knew that. She *was* giving up. In all her 11 years she'd never done that before, not when her mother left, not when the lightning knocked her off a mountain, not when the blizzard ravaged Merrilee's little home in the forest, and not when Joey made it painfully clear he didn't want her around at the start of the camping trip.

The girl began to cry, her sobs weak and painful. "God," she prayed, fists pressed against her face. "I don't want to die in this awful place. Please help me. I'm so cold and scared. The river has taken me, but I want to be home with Daddy and Debbie.

"So I'm going to lie really still and think for a while. If You have any ideas for me, just put them in my mind and I'll get busy doing whatever You say. I promise.

"Grandpa told me that You love every human

being. I just hope You love me even when I'm invisible."

The girl shivered in the darkness, trying to keep her thoughts from giving in to the fear that pressed in on her from all sides. As promised, she lay motionless, letting her mind relax. But something was still wrong. Her knee hurt, throbbing like when she hit it against the corner of her desk in her bedroom. It felt like something was poking into her skin, muscle, and bone.

When she reached down to take hold of her leg and move it, her hand brushed against something smooth and hard. Her fingers recoiled, then relaxed. Dropping her arm, she began searching for the object again. Yes, there it was, resting painfully against her leg.

"What's this?" she asked, rising up on one elbow, sinking deeper into the mud.

Carefully, she groped the strange article like a doctor probes a patient's chest. It was covered with graceful curves and abrupt angles.

All at once, her fingers brushed over some sort of metallic fastener. Part of the object narrowed and had been fed through the cold, hard loop. Wendy's eyes opened wide as a rush of adrenaline shot from head to toe. "I don't believe this," she cried. "I DON'T BELIEVE THIS!"

Reaching out, she grabbed the mysterious object. She lifted it from the mud and pressed it against her chest. "MY SADDLEBAGS!" she shouted, her voice piercing the darkness. "These are my saddlebags. There's food in here, a sweater, gloves, earmuffs, a blanket, and—" She paused mid-sentence as her mouth dropped open. "And matches. There are matches in my saddlebags. I put them there myself back at Shadow Creek Ranch. Stuck 'em in a waterproof container and everything."

Wendy hesitated, suddenly unsure of herself. "But, do I want to know?" she asked. "I mean, what if . . . what if I really am blind?"

She shook her head. "I've gotta find out. I've just gotta."

With energy she didn't know she possessed, the girl drug herself through the darkness, groping her way to a spot that seemed to be a little more out of the water. She gathered her newfound treasure in her lap and fumbled with the fasteners. The first pocket yielded a pair of earmuffs, which she quickly placed over her head. She enjoyed their warm softness against her ears. She discovered a scarf next and soon it was hanging comfortably about her neck.

Wendy was like a child at Christmas, searching with growing excitement for each gift that waited under the tree. Her whole body shook from the cold but she ignored her condition as her hands plundered the hidden confines of her precious saddlebags.

"Plastic wrap," she announced, tearing at an object in her lap. "This must be my peanut butter sandwich." She jammed the remains of a long-for-gotten meal into her mouth, letting the earthy smell and sweet taste flood her body. An apple rose to her lips and splattered her chin as she bit into it. No meal had ever tasted so good. No king who ever lived had savored a feast with such relish as Wendy demonstrated while she joyfully dug first one eatable item and then another from her leather carryall.

Then her fingers struck the cool, smooth covering of the matchbox container. She stopped chewing and stared into the darkness for a moment. "Being blind isn't so bad," she said aloud, her words muffled by the meal bulging in her cheeks. "I mean, I can still taste, and smell, and hear. I just won't be able to see."

She resumed chewing as thoughts bounced around in her head. "Blind people are still people," she reasoned. "They laugh and say stupid things just like everyone else."

Wendy swallowed and brushed apple juice from her chin. "But if I can see, everything will look more beautiful because . . . because I know what it's like to be blind."

Slowly, with great care, she opened the plastic container and felt the box waiting inside. Placing everything safely in her lap, she fumbled for a single match, feeling its rough wooden surface between her cold-numbed fingers. Lifting it, she slowly slipped the box closed and held the two objects out in front of her. "Here goes," she whispered.

With a flick of her wrist, she passed the match

along the side of the box. Nothing. She did it again. Still nothing.

Her fingers explored the small shaft wonderingly. Then she chuckled. "It might help if I tried to light the match on the striking end," she said. This time, when the match brushed against the box, Wendy saw sparks fly out, followed by an almost blinding flash of light. "I can see it," she whispered. "I CAN SEE IT BURNING!"

The sight was almost painful but she held her gaze on the hissing match, watching the white flare soften into a blue and yellow flame. It illuminated the smudged and trembling hand that held it out in front of her. Wendy tipped the little wooden shaft to one side, keeping the flame alive, allowing it to creep slowly toward her fingers.

As she began to feel the heat, she blew softly and the brilliance departed as quickly as it had come. But for the first time since entering her silent domain, she didn't feel that heart-stopping terror press against her. Because now *she* controlled the darkness, and could vanish it with the flick of her wrist.

* * * * *

Dawn was just beginning to tint the eastern sky when Tyler Hanson fell asleep. The long night had passed undisturbed by the man sitting at the lip of the gaping hole in the ground. He'd watched the moon traverse the sky, bending shadows in the forest, offering its silver light as a cold consolation to his breaking heart.

From the moment Justin Stanfield revealed what he hadn't seen, the lawyer knew his daughter was dead, or at least soon would be. Eleven-year-old girls weren't designed to be hurled headlong with an entire river into black, gaping punctures in the earth's surface. They were supposed to be tucked into their sleeping bags, safe from the night and nature's fury.

The other members of the search party had tried to console him with promises of renewed efforts at first light. They'd tenderly patted him on the back, spoken softly of not giving up hope, and how Wendy was a survivor. But how did you survive this?

The lonely hours of listening to the muffled scream of the cataract as it plunged into the darkness below, feeling the earth shake as if it too were frightened by the spectacle, brought no answers to his tired mind and soul.

Finally, with the sounds of the river filling the man's ears, exhaustion washed over him, stripping away his ability to think and even grieve, sinking him into restless slumber. As his eyes closed, his lips moved, uttering simple words to the God he knew hovered near.

When he awoke, the sky was a little brighter, the shadows less dense. Even the trees and rocks had lost their shrouds, revealing their familiar cracked and chipped faces once again.

Mr. Hanson smiled to himself without being aware of it. This was Wendy's time of day. She was always up before everyone else, wandering around alone. It was something she'd done since birth. Even as a tiny baby, she'd be awake to greet the dawn. They'd find her lying peacefully in her crib, staring at the ceiling as if waiting for something to happen.

A sob rose in the man's throat and held itself there, making it difficult for him to breathe. How could there be a dawn without his little girl? How could the sun even think of rising without her eyes to welcome it?

"Wendy," the man whispered, the word lost in the moan of the river. "It's time to get up. Time to put on your slippers and bathrobe and go to the den and sit by the coals of last night's fire. You've got to dream your big dreams and make puzzling plans for the day. Do you hear me? Wake up, Wendy. Wake up."

A random breeze nudged the branches overhead, ruffling the dry, autumn leaves as it passed. Then all was still.

Slowly, falteringly, Mr. Hanson stumbled to his feet and stood looking at the river as it arched over the lip of the hole and plunged into the mist-shrouded darkness below.

"I hate you," he said. "I hate you with every cell in my body. You are evil. You've taken my little girl away from me." He lifted his hand, palm up, and addressed the churning waters, his voice trembling. "Why? Why did you do it? Couldn't you've left us alone? We're a family. We loved each other. Wendy wasn't doing you any harm. She was just trying to

go for help, and you took her without a word." The
man hesitated, grabbing a low limb for support.
"Give her back," he pleaded. "You must give her
back to me so I can take her home to her little room
where she can wake up and greet the dawn. Please,
river. Give her back to me."

There was no answer to his agonizing command,
only the angry voice of the waters speaking words
he couldn't understand.

The lawyer left the edge and walked along the
path that led away from the river. The rising sun
had just begun to chase night from the land, brushing distant mountaintops with golden light and
washing the cloudless sky with a brightening glow.

He'd walked half a mile when the faint scent of
leather touched his senses. A few paces more and
the aroma grew stronger. *Strange*, he thought. He
was still far from the new base camp. There should
be no such odors in the early morning air.

The aroma increased with each passing moment.
Mr. Hanson paused, head tilted slightly, allowing
the mysterious fragrance to saturate his nostrils.

Wait. It wasn't just leather he was sensing. It
was *burning* leather. That was impossible. The
search teams at camp wouldn't be burning anything
of that nature, especially since all the cooking fires
would be cold after the long hours of darkness.

As the man crested a rise in the land he found
himself looking down into a meadow. But what he
saw caused his heart to skip out of rhythm. Rising
like phantoms from the earth, lifting themselves

out of dozens of unseen pockets in the ground, were thin, wispy columns of smoke. They twisted and turned slowly, drifting skyward, mingling with the trees that bordered the clearing, wrapping them-selves around low-lying shrubs like silent, winged serpents. And with each passing moment, the odor of burning leather grew stronger and stronger.

"What's happening?" Mr. Hanson said aloud. "Am I going crazy? What could make such a strange illusion appear in the meadow?" Like a bolt of light-ning arching through the sky, the answer struck him with enough force to take his breath away. Someone at this early morning hour was burning leather below the ground. The smoke from that fire was finding its way to the surface, venting itself through tiny earth chimneys scattered about the meadow.

The man began to run. With leaps and shouts he raced into the clearing, letting the rancid smoke boil about him like currents swirling over rocks. He jumped through the columns, laughing, crying, clapping his hands together in the cold morning air.

Then he stopped, as if suddenly afraid he'd crush something underfoot. Tenderly he knelt and passed his trembling hands over the damp grasses and soil. With great care, he lowered himself to the ground, pressing his face into the cold earth. Dirt stained his lips as he planted a kiss at the very cen-ter of the meadow. "We're coming," he whispered, barely able to speak his promise. "Don't be afraid, Wendy. We're coming."

Hurrying back to the path, he turned once again to stare at the mysterious scene. The agony that had been his companion through the night had loosened its grip, leaving the man almost lightheaded with joy. "I love you!" he shouted, his proclamation racing across the meadow like a leaping fawn. "Do you hear me, sweet Wendy? I love you!"

Then he rushed away, chasing the morning light into the forest.

* * * * *

The fire crackled and snapped, illuminating the large stone chamber with dancing phantoms of light. Wendy sat on a piece of driftwood, watching the flames, letting their warmth seep into her skin. It was a big fire, tossing billows of smoke and spark high into the darkness.

"Hey, river," the girl called as she dropped another gnarled and broken branch into the blaze. "Thanks for the wood. It was kind of you to pile it up so neatly." She chuckled. "Sorry 'bout the smell, but here's how I see it. Smoke's gotta go somewhere. I mean, have you ever seen the geysers spewing out of the ground in Yellowstone? Some areas look like giant steam baths. Red Stone, my Indian friend, calls them spirit valleys. They're neat.

"So I'm thinkin' maybe this cave has some passages to the surface, as well. But—follow me, here—you gotta use your head. If someone topside saw smoke rising from the ground, they'd say, 'Look at that, just like Yellowstone.' Then they'd build a resort and charge an arm and a leg for tourists to come take shaky videos of the new Bob Marshall Wilderness wonder. But, like my daddy says, if you wanna be noticed, you gotta be different. That's why I sacrificed one of my faithful saddlebags to the cause. Smoke coming from the ground? Big deal. Smoke coming from the ground that smells like burning leather? Not your everyday occurrence. At least, I hope not."

The girl tilted her head as if listening to something. "What's that, river? Is anybody looking for me? Well, if Joey escapes the valley in one piece, and isn't too mad at me for wandering off alone, he'll get hold of my dad and they'll sit around shaking their heads, talking about what a stupid thing I did. Then they'll have a big laugh and meander back into the wilderness with a couple bloodhounds and maybe an Indian guide with a strange name to track me down. Of course, they won't find me 'cause I'm stuck down here in this warm and cozy place. But maybe, just maybe, one of the dogs will sneeze and they'll wonder why and start lookin' around. That's when they'll see the smoke that smells like a really hot horse and, bingo, they'll start figuring out a way to get me back to where the sun shines."

Wendy watched the fire for a few moments, then sighed. "Or maybe they won't."

She looked around thoughtfully. "I've got plenty of dry wood down here, thanks to Mr. River and his weird ways. I can keep a fire going for warmth and

85

light, and of course, smoke. Looks like I have food for about three more meals if I don't pig out like I did earlier. Water certainly isn't a problem—Old Man River may be mean, but he's clean. So, all in all, as soon as my head, shoulder, right arm, right hip, left leg, right knee, and both ankles stop hurting, I'll be fine. Oh, yes, my nose. It hurts, too. Feels like Early kicked me in the fa—"

Wendy stopped talking as visions of her horse raced across her thoughts. "Early," she repeated the word softly. "Did you get out of the river in time? Or are you down here somewhere, too?" The girl closed her eyes, replaying the awful scene of her fall. She'd been riding along the riverbank, and suddenly the horse had slipped, tossing her into the rapids. The reins had cut into her palms and fingers as she struggled against the current. Then they'd slipped away. No, she wasn't holding onto the horse when she went over the edge.

"He didn't fall in the hole," she said flatly, without emotion. "He just didn't. Early got away. The river didn't take him. I know that."

Flames cracked and hissed as Wendy moved closer to their warmth. She stirred the red-hot ashes with a long stick and sighed. Where was Early now? Was he OK? Or had the river done terrible damage to her best friend?

* * * * *

A chipmunk busily storing nuts for the coming winter paused in his duties and lay, legs outstretched, on the high limb of an aspen tree. The early morning sun felt good, soaking into his fur and bringing energizing warmth to his skin.

His den, hidden nearby, was almost full of food supplies. But chipmunks never depend on numbers. They work until the snows come and bury them deep underground, out of reach of winter's freezing grip.

A movement on the forest floor startled the little animal, causing him to chirp, chirp, chirp out a warning. He scurried along the limb and hopped onto the trunk of the tree, hanging facedown, skittering about trying to discover what had caught his eye.

Lower, lower, lower he came, keeping up his constant call just in case some other forest creature was unaware of the situation. But, like all wild animals, he was curious. Something had disturbed the forest calm far below and he wanted to know what it was.

As he jumped onto the last limb, his chirping stopped. Below him lay a large animal, unmoving, silent. Other woodland creatures crept forward from among the leaves and branches, peering nervously at the strange sight. They sniffed the air, wiggled their tails, jerked about like they were trying to attract the attention of the still form. But no amount of aggressive behavior seem to rouse the visitor in their shadowy domain.

In a few minutes, all the chipmunks, squirrels, birds, and other animals melted back into the forest. There was work to do. Winter was coming. They couldn't stand around all day gazing at some unmoving pile of skin and hair and expect to be ready when the snows came. No, sir! But they'd check back later to see if the situation had changed.

Little did they know that the stranger in their midst hadn't chosen to spend the night in their forest home. He'd rather have spent the cold hours safe and snug in his straw-carpeted stall on a ranch far from this woodland spot.

Besides, horses didn't belong in the forest. They preferred open spaces, with lots of running room and tender grasses to eat. But this particular animal didn't have a choice right now. Why wasn't he content to lie there, soaking up what sunlight found its way to the forest floor? Because he wanted desperately to leave, to find an open meadow. But he couldn't. For the first time in his young life, he was experiencing a real problem. It was such a mystery that the animal seemed surprised by it.

For some reason, he couldn't get up. Maybe it was the pain in his leg, or his back. Maybe it was the terrible ache throbbing in his hindquarters. Whatever was happening, he didn't like it.

The horse lifted his head and struggled, trying to rock back and forth in an attempt to position his heavy body over his hooves, but he couldn't.

He lay back against the ground exhausted, an angry snort blasting from his nose. What was going on? Why couldn't he jump to his feet and trot away as usual?

The sun spilled random rays through the trees, sprinkling soil and rock with pools of light. But the beauty of the morning was lost on the creatures eagerly going about their business high overhead in the trees, and the large visitor lying prone among the leaves.

* * * * *

Hawk and Grandpa Hanson could see the smoke even from miles away as they roared over the wilderness in the Pacemaker. The pilot pointed, then shook his head. "Right where Tyler said it would be. Wendy's a very resourceful girl."

"That's for sure," his passenger agreed, glancing back to see if the equipment he and Hawk had carefully loaded at the lakeside dock in Polson was still secure. "Of course, her exact location is still a mystery," Grandpa Hanson added. "Smoke can travel a long distance, especially underground where there's little if any wind to disturb it."

"But I think Ranger Perez has the right idea," the pilot stated. "We simply follow the smoke back to where it came from." He nodded to himself. "Yup, that granddaughter of yours is really somethin'."

The Pacemaker banked slightly as the pilot guided it toward their distant destination. He studied the wrinkles and rills in the land and sighed. "We haven't had our talk yet."

"Talk?"

"Yeah. You know. What we were discussing yesterday?"

Grandpa Hanson nodded. "Oh, yes! Hawk, I'm so sorry. Guess my mind was occupied elsewhere."

"No problem," the pilot chuckled. "*I* hadn't even been thinking about our conversation until a few minutes ago. Sometimes, flying this old crate sets my memories in motion. Some of what I see isn't very pleasant."

"You mean the war?" Grandpa Hanson asked.

Hawk nodded slowly. "I was a fighter pilot in Nam. F-4s. That aircraft's a real killing machine."

The old man gazed out the window. "War is never pleasant."

"Were you a soldier?"

Grandpa Hanson sighed. "Sicily. 1944. I was with Patton's Seventh Army, 3rd Infantry Division. We came ashore at Licata and about got our heads blown off."

"Tough, huh?"

The passenger frowned. "I saw things I've never even shared with my wife."

The two sat unspeaking for a couple minutes, listening to the roar of the engine and of long-ago battles.

"I was young and full of myself," the old man continued. "Invincible. Know what I mean?"

Hawk nodded.

"There was this medic with our unit, guy named Rashad. I think he was Arab or something. Born and raised in New York City, same as me. Anyway, while I'm busy throwing hot lead at the enemy, he's runnin' around patchin' guys up, you know, playing doctor in what was rapidly becoming a pretty messy morgue. This goes on for hours. I'm firin' away, he's crawlin' on his belly trying to put people back together again."

"So what happened?"

The old man gazed out the window. "A panzer tank suddenly appears from behind this farmhouse and opens fire. Rashad never knew what hit him. I saw him fall." Grandpa Hanson sighed. "That's war in a nutshell—men and women killing and saving each other, all at the same time."

Hawk glanced at his companion. "But I never saved anyone. It wasn't exactly in my job description." He hesitated. "Do you think God can forgive me for that?"

Grandpa Hanson waited before he answered. When he spoke, his words were hopeful. "I used to think that if only I'd been like Rashad and spent the war saving lives instead of taking them, I wouldn't have to bother God with my feelings.

"But then someone showed me where the Bible says *all* people are sinners and in need of forgiveness. *All* people, even my friend Rashad. So I guess you can't judge how good or bad you are, based on the life of another human being. Doesn't work. You've gotta say to yourself, 'How do I stack up against Jesus Christ?' Believe me, when you compare yourself to Him, you know the Bible's right.

"Instead, you've gotta think, *Do I accept God's sacrifice and forgiveness for my mistakes?* Only then can you feel halfway good about yourself, and look forward to the day ahead."

Hawk lifted his hand. "You mean God forgives us *before* we do something wrong?"

"Yup. Jesus' death on the cross was painful proof of that fact. It's in the Bible."

Hawk rubbed his chin thoughtfully.

"Oh, and one more thing I learned about forgiveness," the old man stated. "Seems it doesn't take into consideration *why* we do something, because if it did, we could all say we're victims and make excuses for our sinful actions. Sin is sin, whether we think it's justified or not. There's never an excuse for breaking one of God's laws. But our heavenly Father wants to help us change our ways, to become a new person."

Grandpa Hanson sighed. "I will always feel sad about what I did during the war, about the enemy soldiers who never went home to their families because I was there. But, since I discovered God's love and chose to change from a hotheaded warrior to a child of heaven who was sorry for his deeds, I feel forgiven, too. Jesus helps me carry my burden of shame so it doesn't crush me."

The old man studied the pilot thoughtfully. "Forgiveness turns guilt into an almost overwhelming desire to spend the rest of your life finding ways to ease the pain of others."

Hawk turned to face his passenger, his eyes reflecting the deep yearning in his heart. "Are you saying that God will forgive me for what I did?"

Grandpa Hanson smiled. "He already has, Hawk. A long time ago."

The bright Montana sun looked down from above as the Pacemaker turned to the left and began a shallow descent toward a ribbon of water far below.

* * * * *

Joey surveyed the scene thoughtfully. Here was a meadow filled with smoke, yet no crackling flames could be seen or heard. It was like a forest fire . . . without the fire.

"How come the wood she found isn't wet?" he asked Ranger Perez.

The man dropped a handful of shovels onto the rocky ground and shook his head, pointing downward with a gloved finger. "River must've changed course under here, leaving driftwood high and dry. Wendy probably stumbled onto a pile and torched it." Ranger Perez paused. "She's one smart cookie."

Joey grinned. "Don't let *her* hear you say that. She'll want it in writing and make copies to pass around to friends and family."

The ranger chuckled. "She sounds like quite a character. I think I'll enjoy meeting her."

"She grows on you," Joey grinned. "Sorta like fungus grows on trees."

"You'll have to excuse the lad," Mr. Hanson called as he joined the two by a particularly smoky bush. "He has yet to appreciate my youngest daughter's more noble traits."

"*Noble* traits?" Joey asked. "Like driving me crazy, or robbing the horse barn of important tools,

93

or 'borrowing' stuff I told her she couldn't have, or sneaking off on her own when I told her to stay put, or—?"

"Yeah, those," the lawyer interrupted with a laugh. He turned to the ranger. "You should see her on a bad day."

Mr. Perez shook his head. "You guys really love that little girl, don't you?"

"Me?" Joey gasped. "Love Wendy Hanson?!" The boy reddened and kicked at a stone. "Well, I guess I do, in an I-can't-believe-I'm-saying-this sorta way. I give her a tough time, but deep down, I mean really *deep* down, she's an OK kid. She does make me laugh, that's for sure."

"Well, Joey Dugan," Mr. Hanson blinked. "I do believe you're going soft on us, admitting your true feelings for Wendy." The man sighed. "This is a real Dear Diary moment."

Joey blushed. "Give me a break."

The two men burst out laughing as they slapped the teenager on the back and returned to work. They knew the subject of their mirth was still somewhere underfoot and needed saving as soon as possible. But it felt good to laugh, after the endless hours of worry and dread. Wendy was alive and kicking. The next order of business was to bring her, in the same condition, back to the surface of the Bob Marshall Wilderness.

* * * * *

"So, how are they going to find her?" Debbie

asked as the Trooper bounced along a rutted log-
ging road a few miles southwest of the sinkhole.

Barry shifted gears, grimacing with the effort.
"They'll try and follow the smoke back to its
source."

"You mean someone's gonna have to go into the
ground?"

"That's the only way to do it."

Debbie shook her head. "That'd be scary, especially knowing how the river can change directions
at any moment. You could be hanging in midair
somewhere and suddenly find yourself trying to
swim up Niagara Falls." She shivered. "Poor
Wendy. They've gotta get to her. If they need volun-
teers, I'll go."

Barry chuckled. "I'll bet you would."

"Me, too," a little voice called from the back seat.
"That river doesn't scare me. No, sir. I'd do anything to save my friend Wendy."

"Good for you, Samantha," Barry smiled. "But I
think you'd better stay with us and try to track
down ol' Early. He must be gettin' kinda lonely by
now."

"Yeah," Samantha nodded. "He misses Wendy,
too."

Debbie glanced at the driver. "We're all doing
our part to help save her," she said. Barry guided
the vehicle around a fallen log and drove on, his
eyes not leaving the rough road.

* * * * *

Wendy had the feeling that someone, or something, was looking at her from the dark shadows beyond the ring of light cast by the bonfire. She wasn't sure; it just felt like it. But when she'd spin around, trying to catch a glimpse of the intruder, all she'd see was empty space, something her underground chamber had lots of.

The room, she figured, was about 100 feet long and maybe 75 feet across. One end was solid rock except for a 10-foot gap that extended from the floor into the darkness above. Her underground home was divided almost in half by a deep, still-flowing channel of cold water. Debris littered the floor—logs, branches, and, most disturbing of all, the skeletal remains of several unfortunate forest creatures who'd been swept into the void by the river in times past.

Fingers of stalactites hung overhead. Directly below them, stalagmites rose from the smooth floor like rows of pointed teeth. Parts of the cave reminded Wendy of sitting inside a large dog's mouth, looking out, something she'd wondered about but thankfully never experienced firsthand.

The channel of water disappeared without a sound through another large crack in the opposite wall. As for a ceiling, the girl figured there had to be one, but she couldn't see it. Not even the light radiating from her fire reached far enough. A pebble plunked into the water some distance away, causing Wendy to jump. "Hey. No throwing stuff!" she called, her voice echoing from many directions at once. "This cave has certain rules, one of which is to not scare me, which you just did, so please leave."

She paused, as if in anticipation of an answer. "Are you what I heard earlier, you know, breathing like someone with a bad case of asthma? Was that you?"

No response.

Wendy edged a little closer to the fire. "I . . . I'll be leaving soon and you can have the whole place to yourself. OK?"

She tilted her head as, from somewhere far away, she heard a new noise, like a tiny portion of a cry.

"Who's there?" the girl demanded. "Come on. You're breaking my most important rule again."

Another pebble slipped from a ledge in the distant darkness and splashed into the still waters. The girl whirled about to face the sound. "I'm warning you," she shouted, her alarm repeated by the cave. "I don't like you sneaking around like this. Makes me really, really nervous."

She reached down and lifted a burning limb from the fire. Slowly, painfully, she stood and moved toward the far end of the grotto, holding the torch above her head. "I didn't ask to be down here," she exclaimed. "I mean, do I look like a bat to you?"

Wendy stepped gingerly around piles of stone and gnarled, shattered tree limbs. "I was just mindin' my own business, trying to ride out of the wilderness, when the river got me. You know the river, don't you? Big? Wet? Runnin' all over the place like a mixed-up Mississippi? Maybe it got you,

DITD-4

too. Is that what happened?"

The light from her flame illuminated the passageway between the towering walls at the far end of the chamber. Wendy squinted into the shadows, trying to make out any forms hiding there. "So, why don't you just come and join me by the fire? We'll tell ghost stories." The girl stiffened. "Oh. I guess I shouldn't have suggested that. I'll tell you about the ranch I live on and you can tell me about . . . about whatever you want to talk about. Is it a deal?" She leaned forward, peering around a large boulder. "Do you hear me?"

In the darkness, some distance down the passageway, two gleaming eyes appeared, seemingly floating in thin air. Wendy froze, unable to move another inch, the torch still held above her head.

The eyes were bright yellow with almost white centers, staring at her without flinching.

"Wh . . . wh . . . who are you?" Wendy breathed, feeling suddenly sick.

From the darkness came what sounded like a deep, trembling growl, followed by a shriek that turned every muscle in Wendy's body to a shaking mass of protein. She wanted to run, but couldn't. All she could do was stare at the eyes, her burning limb held high. "D-d-don't kill me," she mumbled, her tongue suddenly unresponsive. "Pl . . . please, don't kill me."

The eyes floated slightly to the left, then returned to their first position. And as quickly as they'd appeared, vanished.

Wendy turned as soon as the spell of the staring eyes released her and began stumbling back the way she'd come. Her legs didn't seem to want to cooperate, but she forced them through their paces anyway, slamming herself against obstacles, tripping over rocks, careening around slippery boulders, hurrying as fast as her feet could carry her in the direction of the bright, crackling fire at the other end of the chamber. Not only did she now know she had company in her dark, underground home, it possessed evil-looking eyes whose stare robbed her of the ability to move.

Even as she dropped to the ground at the base of her bonfire, her breath coming in painful heaves, Wendy knew she hadn't seen the last of her mysterious companion. All morning she'd worried whether she had enough to eat. It now occurred to her that she might be on the menu of the owner of those eyes. How much time would pass before the creature hiding in the shadows decided he'd waited long enough, that it was time to enjoy the meal the river had dropped at his front door?

CHAPTER 5

Day Two—Afternoon

🐾 🐾 🐾

"OK, everybody, listen up." Ranger Perez wiped sandwich crumbs from his lips with a paper napkin and cleared his throat. He motioned for the remaining members of his search teams to gather around the lunch table for a quick conference before work resumed.

Wrangler Barry, Debbie, and Samantha weren't with the group. Earlier in the day, they'd decided to pack food and camping gear for a final, all-out attempt to overtake the illusive Early, even if that meant eating on the trail and spending the night under the stars. Barry had indicated growing concern over the horse, saying the little stallion might not survive another night in the wilderness. He must be found and given medical treatment. They'd radioed reports throughout the morning, none of them encouraging.

With this in the back of his mind, Ranger Perez had finished his lunch and was summoning the troops for an even more crucial mission—to find

Wendy Hanson.

Morning had been spent preparing for the assault on the underground world. A hole large enough for a person to pass through had been found in the meadow. Smoke drifting from it, carrying the unmistakable scent of burnt leather, indicated a possible passageway to the lost girl. There was only one problem, and that's what the ranger wanted to address at this after-meal meeting.

"As you know, we've rigged a heavy-duty electric winch and sturdy support frame above the meadow hole," he began. "Lucky for us, Hawk had this equipment in working order at his landing site on Flathead Lake. He and Grandpa Hanson flew it in this morning."

Hawk smiled and swallowed the last bite of his sandwich. "Bought it 'bout a year ago when the Pacemaker sunk. Funny story."

"Your airplane sank?" Grandpa Hanson gulped, almost choking on his hot chocolate. "I've flown in that contraption twice!"

"Don't worry," the pilot chuckled. "I pulled it right out of the lake with my new winch. Fixed 'er up good as new, although she still gurgles from time to time."

Grandma Hanson patted her husband's arm lovingly. "Congratulations," she said. "You've now been carried aloft in an aircraft that gurgles. Not everyone can say that."

The old man shook his head. "Well, I guess it's worth it if we can get our Wendy back to the surface sooner." He held his hand over his chest. "It's just kinda unsettling to discover you've been buzzing about the sky in an airplane that used to be sitting at the bottom of Flathead Lake."

"As I was saying," Ranger Perez continued, winking at his older companion, "we've rigged the winch to lower someone into the hole. Just before we broke for this quick lunch, we gave it a test run. Ranger DeMitri put on the harness and gas mask and descended about 20 feet when the passageway got too narrow for him to squeeze through. Looks like we've got to rig another hole. With everyone helping, that shouldn't take more than an hour or so."

"An hour?" Joey called from nearby where he'd been busily stuffing supplies in a small backpack. "That's too long. Now that we know Wendy's alive, we've gotta act fast. No tellin' what the river will decide to do next." He tossed the pack over his shoulder and grabbed his hat. "We gotta go in now."

Mr. Hanson lifted his hand. "Hold on there, Joey. You're not suggesting that we lower *you* into that hole?"

"Why not? I'm the smallest guy here; a fact that doesn't exactly do a lot for my ego. And I'm agile. No offense, Ranger DeMitri. I can squeeze through some pretty small places. You should've seen me in the warehouses by the East River. I could get in and out of a storage loft before Chief Abernathy knew what hit him *and* haulin' a bunch of loot to boot. So I should be the one to go down the meadow hole."

The lawyer shook his head. "No way, Joey. I already have one child in danger. I'm not about to put you in jeopardy as well."

"Come on, Mr. H," the teenager pressed. "I'm not trying to be a hero or nothin'. An hour is a long time to wait if you're stuck underground in some dark cave. And who's to say we'll even find another workable hole this afternoon? This one drops 20 feet, and even farther for me. We can't wait any longer. She's been down there for over two days. Let me go. I want to. Really."

Mr. Hanson closed his eyes, a soft sigh blowing past his lips. "Joey. If anything were to happen to you, I . . ."

"Mr. H," the boy interrupted softly. "That's our Wendy down there. Wendy. She's worth it to me. I know how much you love her. I watch you guys at the ranch, how you look at her with such happiness in your eyes. I see her run to you when she's hurt or frightened, and I think, hey, that's really beautiful. You know what I mean? I gotta get her back so you can take care of her and be her father like before. And . . ." Joey paused, trying to control his own feelings. "And I couldn't imagine Shadow Creek Ranch without Wendy. It just wouldn't be right." He looked into the man's eyes. "She's worth it to me, Mr. H. She's worth it all."

Ranger Perez stepped forward. "It's up to you, Tyler," he said. "The boy could probably get through, but I can't ask him to go down there. That's your decision to make."

Mr. Hanson pressed his fists against his eyes and held them there for a long moment, head bowed. Finally, he looked up and gazed into the eager face of his young friend. "I . . . I really love you, Joey Dugan," he said.

A gentle smile spread across the teenager's face. "Yeah. I know."

Mr. Hanson wrapped strong arms about the boy and held him tightly. "Stay alive," he whispered. "Please, stay alive."

"I will," Joey said, returning the embrace. "Besides, you need me too much. I gotta watch out for you, too. It's my job."

Ranger Perez shook his head slowly from side to side. In all his years of working the wilds of Montana, he'd seen many acts of bravery, usually performed by people trained to put their lives on the line for others. But here was something different, something beyond reason. A young boy from East Village was willing to sacrifice himself simply because of love. And a father was allowing it to happen for the same reason. It seemed that, when experience and training weren't enough, love could extend the search one step farther, even when that step was into the unknown.

"Let's get to the meadow," the ranger invited. "Wendy's waiting."

The group hurried to gather their tools and equipment, calling instructions and reminders to each other. Joey ran to his tent and was zipping up a canvas bag packed with food and medical supplies when he heard a soft, female voice calling his name. Turning, he saw Lizzy standing at the entrance.

"You're doing a very brave thing," she said.

The boy looked away. "I don't feel so heroic right now."

Lizzy entered the tent and let the flap close behind her. "Are you all right?"

Joey shrugged. "I think I'm a little scared, Dizzy."

The old woman smiled. "Brave people usually are."

Neither spoke for a long moment. "I just wish I could've said goodby to Sam," the boy stated. "Will you . . . will you do that for me?"

"Of course."

"And tell Barry . . ." Joey couldn't continue.

Lizzy walked over and placed a hand on the teenager's shoulder. "We'll all be here waiting for you when you return. Then we'll travel back to Shadow Creek Ranch and you can ride Tar Boy through the hills and fuss at Debbie and listen to the wind whispering in the trees once again. And every time you look at Wendy and Mr. Hanson, you'll feel something deep inside that no one else can feel. I'm proud of you, Joey. I'm so very proud of you."

The boy turned and faced his lifelong friend. "So, it's OK that I'm scared?"

"Fear can keep you safe," Lizzy said, "if you use it correctly. Don't give in to it. Don't let it guide you, but make it work on your side. And, Joey, never forget who's there with you, even in the darkness. He's been there before. He'll show you what to do."

Joey nodded and picked up the bag. "You taught me good, Dizzy," he said. "I don't think I ever thanked you proper."

"You're doing it right now," the old woman smiled. "Just remember, no matter what happens, me and God are with you, one in spirit, one in person. And we can save Wendy as long as we stick together."

The boy grinned and took in a deep breath. "Then what are we waiting for? Let's go get that silly girl and bring her back home again. OK?"

"OK."

With a quick hug, Joey hurried from the tent and joined the rest of the team by the vehicles. Lizzy watched him from the entrance, her eyes filling with tears. With a wave and grind of gears, Joey and the others were gone.

The old woman sank to her knees, arms clutched at her chest. "Please, God," she prayed, "bring him back safely to me. Please."

In the meadow, where smoke drifted above autumn grasses, an electric winch waited, ready to lower a brave boy into the most terrifying world he'd ever known.

* * * * *

The scream turned Wendy's blood to ice. She spun around, her back to the fire, holding the carrot she'd been eating out in front of her like a weapon. Something was stirring at the far end of the chamber, something with bright yellow eyes and raspy breath.

It seemed the wait had ended. The creature who lived in the shadows was hungry for fresh meat, and the girl trembling by the fire would serve nicely to appease his growling stomach.

With these thoughts crowding her mind, Wendy stood shakily to her feet. If she was to die, she wouldn't go down without a fight. It was her nature.

"I see you over there," she said, addressing the glowing eyes no more than 50 feet away, at the edge of the ring of light cast by the fire. "If you want me, you'll have to come and get me." Her voice shook like her hands and knees.

The eyes swayed in the darkness.

"I'm not going to just sit around and let you take me, you know." Wendy bent and started fishing through the remaining saddlebag with her free hand. "I can fight, and I will!" She glanced down for just a second, then back up again. The eyes were gone.

"Oh, no, you don't," she shouted, fumbling for something in the bag. "I know your tricks. You want me to think you're gone. But you're still there, just outside the light. I can hear you breathing." The eyes reappeared 15 feet to the left of where they'd been. Wendy adjusted her position, but this time, instead of a carrot in her hand, she held a long hunting knife, its blade reflecting the firelight in cold flashes. "See? Now we're on a little more equal terms, aren't we? Betcha didn't think I had this.

Well, surprise, surprise. No self-respecting camper would venture out into the wilds without a knife in his saddlebag. No, sir. This puts a whole new light on the subject, doesn't it?"

Another shriek pierced the cold air, causing Wendy to draw back impulsively. "I can yell, too," she stated. "Wanna hear me?" She drew in a deep breath and let loose a scream that echoed and reechoed around the big chamber like a rubber ball bouncing about a handball court. "You don't scare me," she lied. "You don't have anything I don't have except maybe a bunch of fangs and stuff, but I've got this knife and can do real damage. So, come on. Take your best shot. Let's get this over with once and for all. Do you hear me? It's gotta end right now!"

She waited, knife twitching out in front of her. The eyes seemed to pause, then began moving forward. Wendy waited, fighting the dizziness trying its best to topple her.

A dark form appeared as the eyes continued their slow approach. The creature was almost in the light, coming closer and closer, creeping through the shadows, about to emerge from the blackness of the cave.

Wendy tightened her grip on the knife and bent her legs slightly, ready to spring to one side should the approaching beast decide to rush her.

The area around the eyes began to brighten, revealing streaks of dark fur highlighted with white lines. A nose broke through the darkness; a flat, whiskered appendage sitting above a small mouth and white chin.

Then the ears appeared, stiffly aiming upward, dark points jutting from their summits.

Wendy's mouth dropped open as the creature moved into the light, dragging its hind legs, stopping occasionally to scream in pain. The knife clanked to the ground as the girl dropped to her knees. It was immediately evident that her attacker could no more do her damage than she could use the weapon against him.

"You're . . . you're a mountain lion," she gasped, her heart seemingly beating in her throat. "A young one. You've been hurt. Oh, you poor thing!"

The creature's tongue hung limply from his furry mouth, dried blood staining his matted and torn chest. He'd pause and shiver as some tortuous pain shot the length of his body, forcing him to scream, venting his agony into the cold cave air. Then the animal would continue his journey in the direction of the girl.

Wendy began to cry, her young heart breaking as she watched the awful scene. But she knew better than to race to the animal's rescue. This was a wild mountain lion, a creature who survived in a violent world by being equally violent, young as it was. It might not understand the girl's intentions, her well-meaning approach. Whatever energy remained in the broken body struggling over the rocks could easily and suddenly turn the young cat into a ball of fury complete with razor-sharp teeth and blindingly fast claws.

All Wendy could do was watch it struggle in her

direction, crying with pain, driven by an iron will toward the warmth of the fire and scent of food.

"It's OK," the girl called tenderly. "It's OK. I won't hurt you." She fumbled in her saddlebag, withdrawing a piece of bread. "Here. Eat this." She tossed it carefully at the animal. "You must be very hungry."

The bread landed softly at the cat's feet. He stopped and sniffed at it, rolling it with his nose. "Go ahead," the girl urged. "It's for you."

The little creature tried to open its mouth, but found the task impossible. Hunger and thirst had swollen his throat and jaws almost shut. Wendy understood. In his condition, he didn't dare approach the channel of water running through the chamber for fear of toppling in and not being able to get back out again.

"I'm bringing you something to drink," she said softly. "Just stay there. I'll get you some water."

The animal hesitated, watching his companion move slowly to the edge of the channel and dip a small cup into the cold, clear water. Then she placed the container on the ground and moved away.

Agonizingly, the mountain lion struggled to where the cup rested and gave it a couple sniffs. The scent of human was so strong he wanted to run, but the lure of the water proved even more powerful. He dipped his tongue into the fluid and held it there. Wendy saw his mouth begin to move, slowly at first, then a little faster, like a rusted, locked hinge starting to feel the effects of fresh oil poured over it.

"That's right," the girl urged. "Drink it. I'll take care of you. There's food here, and a nice warm fire. Don't be afraid. I would never, ever hurt you."

The mountain lion looked over at the girl, his mouth still hovering above the cup, savoring the cool, lifesaving liquid as it seeped into his body. There was something about her manner, the tone of her voice, that soothed him. For the first time since he'd heard her stir in the darkness the day before, he felt the choking fear ease its grip on his heart. She was not a creature to dread. She was not dangerously aggressive.

A moment ago he'd tried to make his attack, to rid the cave of this unwelcome intruder, but now he felt a strange kinship with the animal sitting by the fire, crowned with golden hair and calling comfortingly.

* * * * *

"Easy. Easy! A little more. Just a little more." Ranger Perez lifted his hand and shouted directions to his coworker, Mr. DeMitri, who stood at the controls of the winch fastened to the bed of the National Park Service truck.

The whine from the heavy machine filled Joey's ears as he felt himself being lifted into position above the newly cleared hole in the ground. Smoke drifted from the hole, blowing away at an abrupt angle as the afternoon breezes swept across the meadow. "Joey, you still read me?" Mr. Hanson's voice buzzed in the teenager's ear.

He nodded. "Loud and clear, Mr. H," he said, speaking into the tiny microphone attached to the thin boom that curved down from his ear and rested just in front of his lips. "I feel like an astronaut about to be blasted into space, 'cept I think I'll be goin' in the wrong direction."

The lawyer chuckled, watching the ranger make last-minute adjustments to the harness strapped tightly around the boy's swaying body. He pressed the transmit button and spoke encouragingly. "Now remember, Joey, you'll be in constant contact with us. Just talk, and the microphone will pick up your words. We've got fresh batteries in the wireless pack attached to your belt, and this gizmo is supposed to have a five-mile range. There'll be plenty of light to see by when you switch on your helmet lantern and, just to be on the safe side, there's a spare flashlight in your backpack. Don't do anything foolish down there. Take it slow and easy. Try to follow the smoke back to wherever Wendy is waiting. You've got a fireman's mask with filters to use when you're actually inside the smoke column. You got that?"

Joey lifted a gloved hand and pointed his thumb skyward. "Like I said, I'm not sure if I'm going down into a cave or up to the moon. Ranger Perez thinks of everything."

"Yes, I do," the man tugging at his straps agreed cheerily. "Just use your head and don't play superman down there. You pull this off and we might have a job for you with the Park Service. Interested?"

"No, thanks," Joey chuckled. "Already got steady work, cleaning horse stalls and huntin' lost campers."

"That's basically what we do," Ranger DeMitri stated, slipping a knife into the leather sheath he'd fastened to Joey's thick belt.

Mr. Perez laughed, giving his coworker a friendly shove. "If the going gets too rough, we'll pull you up. You're the boss. From now on, we do exactly what you tell us. Understand?"

"Got it," Joey nodded, extending his hand. "I know you'll take good care of me."

"We sure will," Ranger Perez said, shaking the boy's outstretched palm firmly. "Now, you ready to do it?"

"Ready," Joey announced, reaching up and slipping the gas mask over his face.

Ranger DeMitri hurried back to the truck and, after shooting a quick glance in Mr. Hanson's direction, started manipulating the levers . The man at the radio waved and pressed his transmit button. "Hang on, Joey. It's showtime."

The teenager felt himself rise further into the air, lifted by the thin but strong cable that ran through a block and tackle arrangement attached to the iron A-frame arching overhead. His feet dangled directly over the black, smoking hole. Then, slowly, he began his descent.

Mr. Hanson watched as his young friend was swallowed up by the earth. He knew that, with the mask over his face, Joey wouldn't be able to commu-

113

nicate for the first few minutes, at least until he was clear of the smoke column. So all the man could do for now was watch the spool of cable at the base of the winch spin slowly around and around, feeding inch after inch of line into the dark hole. For a moment, the scene reminded Mr. Hanson of ice fishing, until he realized they were using Joey Dugan as bait. He quickly struck that image from his mind.

Joey found himself suspended in total darkness. He could feel his harness vibrate as the line attached to it continued to lower him into the abyss. The smell of smoke was strong, somehow evading his mask and saturating his nostrils with its pungent odor.

A sudden feeling of panic swept over him, but he tried to ignore it. He quickly discovered that *offering* to do something brave was a whole lot different than actually *doing* it. He tried to concentrate on why he was on such a dangerous mission. Wendy, that's why. If she was smart enough to send a signal to the surface, then he'd be willing to follow it into her dark world.

He felt the walls of the hole pressing closer, brushing against him from all sides. He knew he must be at the spot where Ranger DeMitri had had to stop. Yes, it *was* narrow. Very narrow. The stone face of the passageway rubbed against him, scraping his clothing, grinding its rough texture into his harness, backpack, and knees.

The index finger of Joey's right hand rested on the emergency call button wired to the cable just above his head. If things got too far out of hand, and he was still wearing the mask, all he had to do was press that button and a signal would sound topside, commanding the winch operator to stop the spool. Two squeezes of the device would immediately reverse his direction. Three would confirm his desire to continue going down. Joey waited, finger poised, ready to arrest his descent if the walls pressing in on him proved too close for comfort.

Then, suddenly, he was free, turning slowly in the darkness. The overwhelming odor of smoke was gone too. Only inky gloom surrounded him. He reached up and removed the mask, letting it drop to his chest, where it hung suspended by straps around his neck. With a click, his helmet lantern lit, sending a beam of light far into the void, reflecting off of absolutely nothing. When he glanced up, the beam from his light illuminated the small passageway he'd just emerged from, thick smoke curling into it from one side. Looking down, he was horrified to see he was rapidly approaching the still waters of an underground river.

He grabbed the microphone boom attached to his ear and flipped the device down in front of his lips. "STOP!" he shouted.

Mr. Hanson jumped. "STOP," the lawyer commanded. DeMitri slammed a lever forward just as Joey's feet touched the surface of the stream.

"What's wrong?" the lawyer called.

Joey breathed a sigh of relief. "I almost went swimming. I'm hanging right above some sort of canal or waterway. Don't know how deep it is. I think I see a bank about 15 feet off to the right. Yeah. Kinda sandy. A few rocks scattered about. Maybe if I get to swinging, I can head in that direction." There was a pause. "Yeah. This is working. I'm swinging back and forth, gettin' closer to the bank. When I give the signal, release the cable and I'll drop onto the sand. Wait for my signal."

The men saw the line moving slightly where it dropped into the hole. Without the winch running, Ranger DeMitri could now hear Joey's voice over the tiny speaker mounted on top of the radio. He waited, hand poised on the release lever.

"NOW!" came the command.

The ranger jammed the lever back, disengaging the drive gear from the spool. He saw the cable feed freely into the hole for an instant, then stop. Suddenly, the spool began spinning again, faster and faster. "NO!" he shouted, reaching for the brake. But before he could grab the handle, he watched in horror as the cable spilled over the mouth of the hole. The spool fed the line out, but no more of it was dropping into the cavity.

"HE FELL!" the man shouted, working to stop the rotating spool. "Tyler, he fell!"

Mr. Hanson pressed the transmit button, his hands trembling. "Joey? JOEY?! Can you hear me? JOEY!"

After a long silence, the men heard a weak voice rattle the speaker. "I hear you."

"Joey! Are you all right?"

116

Another long pause.

"Compared to what?"

The lawyer leaned forward. "Compared to being dead."

"Oh," they heard the teenager respond, "in that case I'm doing quite well, thank you."

"What happened?"

Joey looked about him, trying to figure where he was and how he'd gotten there. "I think I missed the bank."

"What?"

He glanced up, the beam of his helmet shining on a dark corridor directly overhead. "I swung too far and fell into another hole beyond the bank. This cave isn't being very friendly."

"Are you all right?" he heard his friend inquire, the voice loud and urgent in his ear.

"I'm fine, just a bit shaken up. There's a passageway off to my left. Think there's even some smoke blowin' around in it. I'm unfastening my harness and will head off in that direction. Sorry for the scare."

"Just be careful," he heard Mr. Hanson call.

Joey stumbled to his feet and checked to make sure all his equipment was OK. Then he began walking in the direction of the wisps of smoke, following the bright beam of his helmet light into the shadows.

* * * * *

Wendy sighed. She lay against a rock, studying her sleeping companion. The injured mountain lion

117

had finally decided to keep her company, though at a distance. His ability to drink and eat had improved, allowing the creature to accept the small amount of food the girl had to offer. The whole encounter had left him exhausted. That, along with the dry warmth of the fire and the steady, soothing words from his human companion, proved too much for him, and he'd fallen into the first restful sleep he'd enjoyed for a long, long time.

"You poor animal," Wendy said softly, watching his furry sides rise and fall methodically. "I know what it's like to be afraid down here in the dark. It's no fun, is it?"

The creature's front paw moved slightly.

"The river really battered you bad. Me, too. So, here we are, a couple of banged up aliens, sitting in a cave waitin' to be rescued. We're going to be rescued, you know. Soon, too." The girl sighed again. "That is, if my dad and Joey aren't too mad at me and decide to leave me down here all winter just to teach me a lesson."

Wendy tossed another small branch into the fire. "But I *learned* my lesson. Really, I did." She paused, watching the flames dance among the ashes and sticks. "I'm not going to be invisible anymore. Being invisible means being alone, even when you're with people. I . . . I don't want to be alone. It's no fun."

The girl leaned her head against the rock. "Sometimes I think I'm smart and know better than other people. Maybe that's true, but not all that

118

often. Other people have brains. They can figure problems out. They can make decisions. But if they make a decision and it's not the same as mine, it doesn't necessarily mean they're wrong and I'm right. It means they do stuff their way and I do stuff my way. Know what I mean? Different doesn't mean wrong. It's often just another way of being right."

The young mountain lion groaned in his sleep as a pain moved through his prone body.

"I hope I'm not boring you," Wendy called softly to her furry companion. "You see, whenever I'm feeling a little scared about something, I tend to talk a lot. Dad says he can always tell if something is bothering me because I chatter like a magpie. That's a noisy bird, just in case you've never heard of it. Well, this cave is kinda creepy, so I gotta gab to keep my spirits up. So forgive me if I bother your sleep."

The animal growled at some dreamed-up enemy and continued snoozing.

"And another thing I've learned is to listen to people who've done something before. Experience makes you smarter. I know that's true because the next time someone says they're lonely or scared, I'll know exactly what they're talking about. I can say, 'Hey, it'll be all right. Just be patient.' That's what I'm telling myself right now, because I'm already experienced in being lonely and scared."

Wendy shifted her position and looked down at her remaining saddlebag. The food was almost gone. Her generosity to her unexpected guest had drained her supplies, leaving her with one more meager meal to be shared. Then both she and the mountain lion would face yet another obstacle in their stark, silent world.

* * * * *

"Talk to me, Joey," Mr. Hanson called, the hand-held microphone pressed lightly against his upper lip. The radio had been quiet for a while, causing him to become concerned.

"I'm making my way down a long corridor," came the staticky reply. "Rough goin', right now. Slippery. Some type of grayish crust all over everything."

Ranger Perez looked up sharply from the map he'd been studying.

"Don't know what it is or where it came from," the boy continued. "Actually gives me a little better traction. Weird."

The ranger walked over to where Mr. Hanson and the others were sitting. He cocked his head to one side, listening intently to the words coming from the radio receiver.

"This whole area is filled with it."

Ranger Perez took the microphone from Mr. Hanson's hand and brought it to his lips. "Joey. This is Perez. Don't make any quick moves. Do you hear me?"

"Why?"

"Just don't. Walk slowly, and try not to shine

your light upward. Keep the beam on the floor of the cave."

"OK."

Joey paused and carefully shifted the weight of his heavy backpack. What was going on? Why didn't the ranger want him to shine his light up? And where did all this gray-colored crusty stuff come fr—?

Before the question had time to finish in his mind, he felt his foot slip. He fell forward, landing hard on a pile of rocks. Unable to stop himself, he flipped over on his back, the beam from his helmet sweeping the high stone ceiling of the cave like a searchlight brushing the bottom of an overcast.

At first nothing happened, then it seemed the inside of the cave simply exploded. Joey screamed as a million eyes blinked open and dropped straight at him, filling the cold air with the sound of beating wings and a deafening mix of chirps, whistles, and clicks.

"JOEY!" Ranger Perez shouted into the microphone. "Stay calm. Don't move."

"Whadda ya mean, don't move?" the boy cried. "I'm being attacked."

"No, you're not! You just startled 'em. Lie still!"

"What's attacking him?" Mr. Hanson shouted. "What's startled?"

Ranger Perez glanced up, concern in his face. "Bats," he said. "Joey has stumbled into a large colony of cave bats. That's what made the white crust. It's their droppings, called guano, and by the sound of his description, there're thousands of 'em down there."

Joey felt leathery wings beating against him, battering him without mercy. He screamed again, trying to ward off the attack with kicks and desperate swings of his arms.

"Joey, lie still!" the ranger repeated. "Don't move. Do you hear me?" Obediently, the teenager forced his legs and arms to stop their wild thrashing, dropping them lifeless against the coated stones. Even with his eyes tightly closed, he was fully aware of the small creatures fluttering all around his body, snagging his clothes, battering him with powerful wings, shrieking high-pitched warnings into his ears.

The noise reached topside through his tiny microphone. Mr. Hanson gasped, clutching the ranger's arm. "What're they doing?" he cried. "What're they doing to Joey?"

"Probably nothing," the ranger encouraged. "They're just investigating an intruder. If Joey lies still, they'll decide he's harmless and leave him alone."

The lawyer grabbed the microphone. "Be harmless, be harmless," he called.

Joey blinked. What did *that* mean? "I'm lying still, like you told me," he said. "But I'm about to freak out!"

The group waited. A minute ticked by, then another.

Finally a trembling voice sounded from the boy. "They're gone," he said. "And I'm OK."

Mr. Hanson slumped onto his folding chair exhausted. He smiled weakly at the rangers, then lifted the mike to his lips. "Are you sure you're not hurt?"

"I'm fine," came the quick reply. "But that was really unpleasant. If those bats are the warm-up act, I can hardly wait for the main attraction."

The lawyer's face creased into a tired grin. "Hang in there, partner. Let's hope there're no more surprises waiting for you down there."

"Amen to that," Joey called, then added, "Guess I'd better continue. But you'll have to forgive me if I don't do a lot of sightseeing, like stopping to study the cave ceiling."

"Only if you come across another guano field," Ranger Perez counseled.

Joey nodded and rubbed his sore legs. He stumbled to his feet, keeping the beam of his helmet pointed floorward. With an uncontrollable shudder of his shoulders, he moved away, maneuvering around piles of rocks and clutches of stalagmites.

The men topside let out a collective sigh and shook their heads, glad that the search had resumed and Joey was, hopefully, getting closer to the spot where the all-important smoke was being created.

* * * * *

An hour had passed since the mountain lion's afternoon siesta. Wendy's constant assurance and soothing voice had calmed the creature further, drawing him closer to her side.

Now he lay by her legs, allowing her to brush gentle fingers over his tired, emaciated body. This was a new experience for both human and beast, but the shared fear of the cave had driven them together, forming an unusual but powerful bond between them.

Suddenly, Wendy stopped talking. Had she heard something? Even the mountain lion looked up from his dried piece of bread and stared into the darkness beyond the gap in the wall just past the firelight. The girl listened for a minute, then shrugged. "We're hearin' things," she said. "Going bonkers does that to you." She returned to her carrot stick and bit into it, chewing slowly. "This is our last meal," she announced, holding the morsel up in front of her. "If you can call it that. After this, we eat bark."

The mountain lion sniffed the bread and took a delicate bite. He chewed painfully, glancing up at the girl beside him.

Clunk.

The girl and animal both turned to the gap, faces frozen in mid-chew.

". . . ndy . . . ndy . . . ndy."

Wendy blinked. "What was that?"

". . . endy . . . endy . . . endy."

"HEY!" she shouted, causing the lion to flinch. "HEY! We're over here. OVER HERE!"

". . . ere . . . ere . . . ere . . . are . . . are . . . are . . . ou . . . ou . . . ou . . ."

"What?"

". . . ere . . . ere . . . ere . . . are . . . are . . . are . . . ou . . . ou . . . ou . . ."

The girl recognized the tone of the echo, although she couldn't decipher the words. "Joey? JOEY? Is that you?"

"Where . . . re . . . are . . . are . . . ou . . . ou?"

"Here! Joey, we're here!" She turned to her companion. "That's Joey Dugan, the weird guy I was telling you about. He's going to save us."

Jumping to her feet, she hobbled to the gap and peered into the darkness. Far away she could see a light bobbing about, as if bumping into unseen objects. "Joey? Can you hear me?"

". . . endy . . . endy? Is . . . is . . . that . . . at . . . you . . . ou?"

The girl giggled. "No, Joey, it's Elvis. Of course, it's me. Is my daddy with you?"

"No . . . oh. He's . . . too . . . oo . . . ig . . . ig."

Wendy blinked. "My daddy didn't come to save me 'cause he's a pig?"

She heard someone laugh in the darkness. "No . . . oh. He's too . . . oo . . . big . . . ig."

"Oh," the girl nodded. "He's too big. Gotcha."

The light drew nearer. She could make out the form of her friend stumbling through shallow water. And then his sweaty, smudged, and tired face appeared at the gap, firelight reflecting off his broad, ear-to-ear grin.

Wendy quickly hobbled over to him and jumped into his arms, almost toppling them both. Then she pushed herself away, embarrassed by her uncharacteristic outburst of affection. "Hello, Mr. Dugan," she said, clearing her throat. "How are you?"

Joey shook his head and laughed. "I'm fine, Miss Hanson. How're you?"

"I've been better," the girl grinned, her excitement almost bursting from every pore in her body. "You wouldn't happen to have any food in that backpack of yours, would you?" she asked.

"Enough to feed a lion," Joey announced.

"I'm glad to hear that," Wendy giggled, stepping aside, allowing her new guest to see the creature lying by the fire.

Joey's face turned from happy to horrified. In one smooth motion, he grabbed his hunting knife from his belt and held it out in front of him, pushing Wendy aside.

"NO!" the girl called, laying her hand on the outstretched arm. "He's my friend. He's injured. Monty couldn't hurt you if he tried to."

"Monty?"

"Yeah," Wendy said, moving slowly to the fire and resting her hand on the young cat's head. "I named him that. He's been keeping me company down here. See? He's my friend."

The mountain lion snarled half-heartedly at the boy, then lay his head against the girl's foot. "Monty is lost, just like me. He needs saving, too."

Joey let out a deep breath and returned the knife to its sheath. "Why doesn't all this surprise me?" he asked with a tired grin. Then he paused, tilting his head slightly. "Yes? Yes. I'll let you talk to her."

"What are you doing?" Wendy asked, unsure of her friend's strange conversation with no one. The boy removed the earpiece and boom and held it out toward Wendy. "It's your dad. He wants to talk to you."

Wendy's eyes opened wide. "I can speak to him from here?"

"Yes."

She walked over and gently took the earpiece in her hands. Joey could see the girl's false bravery drop like an old garment. Suddenly, she was just a hungry, little lost child deep in a dark cave, about to speak with the man who meant everything to her.

"Daddy?" she said softly, pressing the device into her ear.

Joey saw her eyes fill with tears. "Yes, Daddy. I'm all right. Really."

The boy smiled, delighting in the joy that radiated from the dirt-stained face of his young friend. "No, nothing's hurt bad. But I got scared. I thought . . . Yes . . . I know you love me. And I miss you, too, Daddy. I'm sorry that I . . . I didn't mean to . . ."

The boy looked about the cave, trying to imagine the horror of waking up in such a dark, frightening place all alone, without communication with the outside world. He saw the remains of the burnt saddlebag, the scattered fragments of the girl's last meal, and the many footprints on the chamber floor. She'd survived for more than two days in the underground dungeon, alone, lost in a world of silence and fear. It was more than he could comprehend how she could have made it, much less had the presence of mind to create a signal for someone to follow.

And, of course, there was Monty.

"Yes, Daddy. I will . . . OK . . . I love you too, very much." Wendy handed the communication device to her friend and walked slowly to the fire. With a choked sigh she lowered herself to the cave floor and sat running her hand across the mountain lion's matted fur.

"What's wrong?" Joey asked, slipping the heavy pack off his back and setting it down gently on the stones.

Wendy looked up at him. "It's Early. Dad says they found him."

"And?"

The girl lowered her gaze. "Wrangler Barry says he may not make it. Dad says not to worry, but I know better. Early's going to die. I just know it."

"Oh, Wendy, I'm sorry. I'm so sorry."

The light from the fire flickered about the chamber, casting shadowy figures on the stone walls. But its warmth was lost on Wendy. Although she knew she'd probably be saved, her best friend in all the world was, right now, at this moment, fighting for his very life, and she couldn't be there to whisper words of encouragement and love in his ear.

Danger in the Depths

"A what?" Grandpa Hanson blinked in disbelief as he listened at base camp to the radio message coming in from the meadow.

"They're going to try to bring a mountain lion out with them," the caller repeated.

"You mean a real live, pointy-eared, big-clawed, sharp-toothed mountain lion?"

"You got it."

The old man shook his head. "If it was anyone else in that cave, I'd be surprised. But with ol' Wendy down there, I should've expected something like this."

He heard his son chuckle. "They say they've got it all figured out. When they get to the shafts leading up and out of the caves, Joey's going to fasten himself into the first harness and lead the way. He'll rig Wendy in the second restraint. She'll carry the critter in her arms during the climb, leaving our assistant wrangler to work the cable. Joey's not exactly thrilled with the idea, but he said Wendy wouldn't leave the cave without Monty."

"Monty?"

"The mountain lion."

"Oh, yes."

"So," Mr. Hanson continued, "they're heading back now, following the smoke trail. According to the time Joey spent getting there, we figure he must have gone just several hundred yards before finding our missing girl. But I think everything's going to be fine. Wendy and her feline friend were fed some high-energy food and Joey grabbed a short rest. They're on their way, and not a moment too soon, as far as I'm concerned. This ol' daddy's heart can't take much more."

"Mine either," Grandpa Hanson agreed. "We're all breathing a little easier. Let's just get them up into the sunshine as quickly and safely as possible."

"We're workin' on it," Mr. Hanson announced with growing confidence. "Check back with you later. Meadow out."

"Base out," the old man called.

"Wow," Hawk gasped as he stood to his feet, shaking his head in wonder. "The guys in Polson aren't gonna believe this." He kicked at a pebble and smiled. "Mr. Hanson wants me to stick around and fly our little Miss Zookeeper back to civilization. Says he wants a doctor to check her out and make sure she's OK. I think I'll tidy up the inside of the ol' Pacemaker for my very special passenger. This flight will be a pleasure."

Grandpa Hanson grinned broadly. "I'll help. Nothin's too good for Wendy."

The two men started for the river, where the Pacemaker had been docked by the shore. As they approached, Hawk's brow furrowed. "Oh, brother," he sighed. "Looks like one of my floats has sprung a leak. Bird's tilted to one side. But, not to worry. I've got a sump pump for just such a predicament. Happens all too often with these old pla—"

The pilot stopped dead in his tracks. "Wait a minute. That float isn't leaking. The other one's out of the water, resting on the rocks. What's going on?"

He and his companion hurried in the direction of the plane. "Hey," Hawk said, eyeing the situation. "I didn't taxi the aircraft half up onto the bank like this. I left it out a ways like I always do when the shore's a bit rocky."

Grandpa Hanson took hold of his friend's arm. "Hawk. Your aircraft didn't move. The water did. See? The soil is wet clear up to here." He looked around, sudden concern shadowing his face. "It's the river. I believe it's drying up."

"You're right," the pilot breathed. "And if it gets any worse, I won't be able to leave. I've gotta have open water that's deep enough for my takeoff run. We'd better push the Pacemaker out into what's left before it's too late."

"Grandma! Lizzy!" the old man shouted in the direction of the camp. "Come. We need help."

The two women emerged from the tents and stood looking down at the river.

"Hurry!" Grandpa Hanson shouted. "There's no time to waste."

* * * * *

"Slow down," Wendy groaned, stumbling along behind her companion. "I can't go very fast. My whole body hurts."

Joey paused in the passageway, shifting the weight of the cat that lay wrapped around his shoulders and neck like a thick, furry shawl. "Sorry," he grinned. "I guess I'm too anxious to get out of this creepy place. I'll be glad when we get to the vertical part of our journey. The winch can do all the work then. And *you* can carry ol' Monty." He glanced down at the animal. "I'd hate to have to lug him around if he'd been eating regularly."

Wendy nodded, running her hand along the wall for support. "Those sandwiches you brought helped us both feel a lot better," she said. "Monty liked the lettuce and tomato ones best."

"A vegetarian mountain lion," Joey chuckled. "Grandpa will be pleased."

The girl smiled. "I've got a feeling once we get him out of here and get him well again, he'll make some changes in his menu. Nothin' like a good rodent after a long day in the forest."

Joey nodded, studying the whiskered face resting by his right ear. "How come Monty's so friendly? Aren't Montana mountain lions supposed to be afraid of people?"

Wendy shook her head. "I guess he knows we're trying to help. Believe me, he wasn't so friendly earlier today, but I assured him he didn't have anything to worry about."

"You *assured* him? He understands what you say?"

The girl rolled her eyes. "Well, of course he does. Every word. He's a smart critter."

Joey grinned at the furry face. "Hey, Monty. Who's your favorite football team?"

The big animal snarled and gave a good approximation of a scream. Joey flinched, then nodded. "Montana State University," he said.

Wendy giggled. "That would be the Bobcats, right?"

Joey headed down the dark corridor. "Monty's a very smart pussy cat."

"Don't call him that."

"You mean pussy cat?"

"Yeah."

"Why?"

"He doesn't like it."

Joey addressed the mountain lion. "You don't like to be called pussy cat?"

The animal snarled.

"You're right," Joey gasped.

The two travelers moved into the shadows, following the beams of their lights and were soon swallowed up by the cave.

* * * * *

Justin Stanfield laid his paintbrush down and let out a deep sigh. His wrist was sore. So were his eyes—a result of too much concentrated work at his canvas, doing the same, repetitive action endlessly for hours. But trees needed leaves and meadows demanded carpets of grass.

He could have splashed them on by the square inch, using a big brush and lots of green and yellow paint, but this rendering was unique. He wanted the forest and broad clearing to have as much detail as possible, even if that meant drawing individual leaves and grass stems with painstaking care. Nothing was too good for the little girl and brave teenager who would soon emerge from under the meadow represented in his painting.

But at this particular moment, Justin was experiencing another pain often attributed to artists. It was deep in his belly and was proving quite unpleasant as well as persistent. The man glanced at his watch. "Hey, it's the middle of the afternoon and I didn't have any lunch. No wonder I'm hungry." He quickly slipped the moist illustration into a protective carrying case, folded his easel, and laid his brushes in the paint box. Then he hurried away, shuffling down the trail that led back to his cabin above a roaring river.

As he neared the familiar rocks and stands of pine that comprised his neighborhood, he had the unsettling feeling that something wasn't quite right. The sun was shining as it usually did, backlighting the canopy of leaves high overhead. The smell of broken grasses underfoot filled his nostrils with their sweet scent as they usually did. No, it wasn't the sights and smells of his peaceful portion of Montana that was missing. It was something his ears *weren't* hearing that made the man pause in the path and tilt his head slightly to one side.

It was quiet. Too quiet.

The artist jumped forward, allowing his load of painter's tools and supplies to drop unceremoniously to the ground. Bursting from the tree line, he stood looking down into a dry gully, filled with boulders, dead tree limbs, and nothing else. The cabin hung overhead, oblivious to the fact that the river that had been flowing below, the very stream that had carried the little structure three miles downstream and jammed it violently into the rocks—this same river had vanished, leaving smoothed stone faces as the only reminder of its passing.

Justin Stanfield's mouth dropped open and all color drained from his face. Wordlessly he whirled about and began running, stumbling, along the forest path, his trembling hands brushing aside lowlying limbs and thorn-guarded bushes. His worst fears were being realized. The nightmare was beginning again.

Mr. Hanson and the group of rescuers gathered about the radio transmitter looked up from their work to see a wildman racing across the meadow in their direction, arms waving, voice calling out in a shrill tone.

"What's his problem?" the lawyer asked, standing to his feet.

"He looks upset," Ranger Perez joined in.

"That's not upset," Mr. DeMitri countered, concern edging his words. "He looks scared to death."

But something else caught the abrupt attention of the men by the radio. Every time one of Justin Stanfield's boots slammed into the ground, a spray of liquid shot out from each side, tiny droplets that shimmered in the afternoon sun. With horror the group suddenly realized that the lower portions of the meadow were filling with water.

* * * * *

"Where'd they go?" Joey asked, studying the cave ceiling thoughtfully. He and Wendy were standing in the middle of an area of flat rock covered with a thick gray crust. But the creatures who created the guano field had disappeared completely. Not one little body hung overhead, ready to drop on unsuspecting passersby.

"There were millions of 'em," the boy gasped. "Millions."

Wendy shook her head. "Beats me." She pointed her flashlight at her watch. "It's only 4:00. Don't bats wait until evening to come out and then hunt during the night?"

"Yeah," her companion nodded. "They should still be here, looking down at us with their evil little eyes. Maybe I scared them away."

Wendy chuckled as she rubbed her aching legs. "*You* scared *them* away? You may be ugly, Mr. Dugan, but not enough to frighten a million bats."

The boy grinned. "Why, that's the nicest thing you've ever said to me."

Wendy's brow creased. "Maybe they know something we don't."

"Whadda ya mean?"

"Maybe they heard something, or smelled—" The girl snapped her fingers. "Yeah. That's it. They got fed up with sniffin' my stinky smoke and went elsewhere to hang around for a while. Makes sense, doesn't it?"

Joey shook his head. "Perhaps. But I don't think we'd better stick around to test your theory. Let's keep moving."

The two had gone about three paces when Wendy's hand shot up. "Wait. Do you hear something?"

Joey listened. "No."

The girl turned and gazed in the direction they'd come. She shone her flashlight down the dark tunnel, trying to peer through the inky blackness. "I hear something. Kinda like a roar."

Joey stepped forward. "Wait a minute. I hear it too. And it's gettin' louder."

Wendy maneuvered closer to her friend. "Whadda ya think it is?"

The ground began to shake as if it too was frightened by the approaching sound.

"Let's get outta here," Joey breathed.

"I'm right behind you," Wendy announced, giving a final glance over her shoulder.

At that instant, a wall of seething, churning water burst from the darkness, hurling headlong in their direction. Wendy screamed as Joey grabbed her with his free hand and pressed her against the side of the cave.

The flood swept past, breaking off chunks of rock and debris, its thunder filling their ears with a deep, angry wail.

"Hold on!" Joey shouted as the onrush slammed into their legs. The two fought to keep their balance, straining to press themselves against the rough stone walls of the passageway. What had been a silent, dark corridor had suddenly become a channel rapidly filling with powerful currents.

"It's the river!" Wendy screamed, her eyes glazed with terror. "Joey. It's the river. And it's found us!"

* * * * *

"Wendy! Joey!" Mr. Hanson shouted into the microphone, his voice shrill with concern. He'd just returned from a quick inspection of the meadow and, sure enough, the area was beginning to fill with water.

"Mr. H!" Joey responded as the call rattled in his earpiece. "We've got big trouble down here. The cave is flooding."

The lawyer's face paled. "It's happening up here, too," he announced. "Where are you?"

"In the guano field," Joey reported.

"Can you keep moving?"

"I think so. There's a little space along the side of the corridor. But one slip and we're bass bait."

"Listen to me, Joey," the man urged, his hands

shaking. "Try to get back to the cable. You've got to get there as soon as possible. Do you understand? Don't change course unless you absolutely have to. You could get completely lost and we wouldn't know where to look."

"It's not far to the shaft," the teenager replied. "Maybe 15 minutes, 20 at the most."

"OK, OK. Just be careful!"

There was a pause. "What's happening, Mr. H?" the boy asked.

"I'm not sure," his companion replied. "We think the river is changing course again. Justin says it's dry below his cabin and we've got water in the meadow."

"In the meadow?" Joey gasped. "That'll be right above us."

"Don't you think I know that?" Mr. Hanson shouted. "There's no time to try to figure this out. Keep moving, Joey. Hurry! And tell Wen- y th- t I lo- -er."

The boy heard the man's call crackle, then fade away into silence.

"Mr. H? Mr. H?"

Nothing.

He wiggled the earpiece and boom. "Joey to meadow. Joey to meadow. Do you read?"

Silence.

The teenager reached up and tore the device from his face. "We've lost contact with the surface. And they've got river problems up there, too. Looks like we're on our own."

Wendy took hold of the boy's hand. "Are we going to die? Are we going to die?"

"Not if I can help it," the teenager said firmly, starting to edge along the corridor, his boots loosening stones and hurling them into the rushing water just below. "We've gotta get back to the cable. I can signal them to raise it, even though the transmitter's dead. We've got it hard-wired. Ranger Perez's idea."

Wendy hurried as best she could, following her guide along the slippery ledge.

* * * * *

"We've got to get Hawk into the air," Mr. Hanson called, pressing the transmit button. "Base, do you read? Base?" He gritted his teeth in frustration. "We've lost contact with everyone," he said.

"Batteries are shorting out," Ranger DeMitri called from nearby. "We had the lines running over the ground and the rising water has fried 'em. Nothing I can do about it now."

"Head for base camp," Ranger Perez instructed one of his workers. "Tell Hawk what's goin' on. Get him into the air right now!"

The man nodded and ran to his waiting four-wheel drive vehicle. He sped away across the meadow, throwing up a tail of mud and sending geysers of sparkling spray out over the grass.

"Listen, everyone," the ranger called. "We've gotta get the winch and frame more secure before Joey and Wendy reach the cable. Find big rocks and

140

pile them around the support legs. Hurry! I don't know how far under this meadow's going to go, but I'm not about to second-guess the river. Make it so that the frame won't budge even if it's half submerged. Move the winch truck closer to the hole and toss rocks into its bed. We've got to weight that vehicle down."

Perez's men began running to and fro across the meadow, their boots splashing in the deepening mud, searching for stones and any other heavy objects they could find.

Mr. Hanson and the ranger ran to the winch truck and carefully backed it up until the rear bumper touched two of the support poles that formed one side of the A-frame.

"If the water gets above the tailgate," Ranger Perez called, "it could short out the winch's batteries. Let's add wire and put the power supplies inside the cab and roll up the windows. That'll keep them dry a little longer."

Even as the men worked, they were aware that the water level in the meadow was rising rapidly. As they dropped the last heavy stone into the truck bed, the men found themselves wading almost ankle-deep in a cold sea. Luckily, the hole was situated on a slight rise. That would delay the arrival of the water level to the hole, giving the two children a few more precious minutes of time to get to the surface. If the water reached the lip of the hole before Joey and Wendy escaped, their doom would be sealed.

"That's all we can do for now," Ranger Perez announced, after a few more minutes of backbreaking labor. "Everybody get to the tree line. I'll stay on the truck bed with the winch controls and wait for Joey's signal."

"No," Mr. Hanson responded, jumping up onto the vehicle. "I'll stay. You go."

"Tyler," the man smiled, trying to sound encouraging. "It's going to be OK."

"You don't know that," the lawyer countered. "Besides, those are my children down there. I've gotta be the one to bring them up. They'll want me to be here." He paused. "I have to be here."

Ranger Perez studied the man's face for a long moment. "All right," he said. "I understand. But . . ."

"Yes?"

"Anything can happen, Tyler. The water may rise above the hole. The current could pick up speed and—" He shook his head. "The river can't be trusted. It doesn't care who gets in its way."

Mr. Hanson nodded. "I know. But I've got to try. I allowed Joey to go down there. He's trusting me to help bring him back alive."

The ranger reached out and shook his friend's hand. "We'll be praying for you, Tyler."

Mr. Hanson smiled bravely. "I have a feeling God's going to have a lot to listen to in the next few minutes."

Perez nodded, then gave the equipment a final once-over. As he hopped down from the truck bed he landed in water up to his knees. And, most disturbing of all, the water was in motion, making standing difficult. He glanced back at the lawyer.

"I see it," Mr. Hanson said. "You'd better hurry and get to the safety of the tree line. Ground's a lot higher there."

The ranger smiled, then stumbled away, leaving Mr. Hanson perched on the rocks in the truck bed. The lawyer's hands rested on the winch controls, his eye stared up at the little signal light fastened to the top of the frame.

* * * * *

"Joey, I'm scared," Wendy cried, her words trembling.

The teenager grabbed her hand and half dragged her along the dark passageway, his own feet slipping ever closer to the roaring rapids. "Just a little farther," he shouted.

Their entire underground world had been transformed from a dark, silent void to a roaring, shaking chamber of horrors. Churning water swept past, inches from their boots. Rocks and debris fell all around with sudden deep rumbles and ear-numbing crashes. But above the roar and the shaking, Joey made his voice heard, shouting encouragement and directions.

"This way! Come this way! I remember those rocks. I passed them on the way in. Look, there's soot on the ceiling. Yes. We're getting closer! It won't be long now!"

Monty the mountain lion, wrapped securely

143

around the boy's shoulders, watched the goings-on with fearful confusion, ears pressed flat against his head. What was happening?

Every once in a while he'd glance back at Wendy and see her struggling along, trying to keep up. Was this some sort of game they were playing? Or were they all in terrible trouble? Things weren't exactly peaceful and calm at this moment, what with rocks dropping like bombs and water thundering everywhere. Something was really, really awry here.

But the young cat had learned to trust the creature with the golden hair, and she seemed to place her confidence in the boy who, even now, was carrying him through the endless caverns and corridors. The animal figured he'd leave well enough alone and not make a scene until this wild, peculiar adventure had ended.

"THERE IT IS!" Joey shouted, pointing to a distant cable hanging above a rocky ridge. "See, Wendy? That's our ticket to sunshine."

The girl staggered along behind her leader, her breath coming in painful heaves. Yes, she saw the cable. It sure looked thin.

In moments, Joey was wrapping a leather harness about her, shouting instructions as he worked. "Listen carefully, Wendy. There're two parts to this ride. First we gotta get through that crack up there. See it?" He leaned back, letting the light from his helmet illuminate a small cleft in the cave's stone ceiling. "You're gonna have to walk up the wall, using your legs to keep you from being dragged.

You gotta walk it. Do you hear me?"

The girl nodded.

"Then, when you get above that crack, you'll be in a very big chamber, like where I found you. Just let your body go limp. Hang loose, like a rag doll. It's straight up from there. Let the cable do all the work from there on. You got that?"

Wendy's body was shaking.

"Come on, Wendy. You got that?"

"Y . . . yes."

"Good. I'll go first to deflect any falling debris. You'll be hanging right behind me. And as soon as we get to the surface, I'll unlatch your harness and that'll be that. We're home free."

Joey gently slipped Monty from his shoulders and laid the trembling animal in Wendy's outstretched arms. "Hold on to him tight," he said. "He may try to escape, but don't let him. He'll just fall into the water and get carried away. We don't want that to happen, do we?"

Wendy shook her head no.

"That's right," Joey urged. "We'll save him. I promise."

The grotto shuttered violently as another wave slammed against a wall 100 feet back. Joey gasped as he saw the water level at their boots drop as the wave approached. It sucked all the water from the surrounding channels to build itself into a mammoth, rolling curtain of destruction.

With a quick motion, Joey connected his harness to the cable and pressed the emergency call button.

"HANG ON!" he cried.

Mr. Hanson saw the light flash. His hand jerked forward, slamming the lever against its stop. With a whine, the winch began to spin the spool. Cable immediately started feeding out of the hole. And by the way the machine strained, he knew the line was lifting something heavy. "Come on, Joey. Come on, Wendy," he breathed.

Wendy saw her companion levitate, feet swinging past her face. Then she felt herself jerk upward. At that moment, the wave hit with such force it knocked all the air from her lungs. Her arms tightened around the mountain lion as it struggled to free itself from the creature it now feared was trying to drown it.

She waited in the dark, swirling, crushing swarm of water, her mind repeating the phrase "God? Do You see me? God? Do You see me?"

Joey glanced down past his feet and was horrified to discover Wendy was nowhere in sight. All he could see below him was a churning mass of dark water, screaming its angry curses at him, slapping his face with powerful sprays.

But the line was taut. That meant the girl's harness was holding.

He felt the wall begin to rub his hands and shoulders. Instinctively, he pushed out from the stones, using his legs to keep him off the rough surface.

"Wendy!" he shouted. "WENDY!" The girl popped from the water as the wave roared past, leaving her dangling in midair. "Walk the wall," Joey screamed. "WALK THE WALL!"

Wendy slammed into the wall, almost losing her grip on the animal pressed hard against her chest. Her knees ground into the wall, its jagged edges cutting deeply into her skin.

With a powerful kick, she managed to place her feet and legs into position. With a moan of effort, the girl began walking straight up the fracture, doing her best to follow the directions shouted by the boy above.

And then the wall fell away, leaving her hanging in space. "Now, just relax," Joey instructed. "Don't fight it. It won't be long."

Mr. Hanson felt the truck jerk slightly and glanced to his left. In horror he saw that the meadow was no longer a peaceful, quiet grassland, but from tree line to tree line had become a churning river, tossing swirling, vicious waves at him from all directions. Most heart-stopping of all was the sight of the water cresting the lip of the hole. As it tumbled in it made a sickening, sucking sound.

The winch strained and whined, gears spinning, grinding, shrieking.

Joey looked up and couldn't believe his eyes. "Hang on, Wendy," he shouted. "Looks like we're going swimmi—" His message was cut short by the cascading waterfall. The next instant Wendy found herself enveloped once again in cold, pounding currents. She held her breath, cheeks puffed out, eyes closed tightly. This time the mountain lion didn't squirm. She felt it still and heavy in her arms.

"Come on. COME ON!" Mr. Hanson cried, watching the hole. The cable jerked slightly as the river swirled about the opening, hurling gallon upon gallon into the gap in an all-out attempt to plug the cavity.

Suddenly, through the spinning whirlpool beginning to form around the lip of the hole, there emerged a hand, then another, followed by arms and Joey's flushed and bruised face.

"JOEY!" the man shouted. "You're out! YOU'RE OUT!"

The boy opened his eyes and blinked.

"Unfasten your harness! Grab one of the supports and wait for Wendy."

The teenager did as he was told and adjusted his position on the A-frame, ready to help his companion the moment she appeared.

The structure began to lean to one side as the truck slipped toward the hole.

"Oh, NO!" Mr. Hanson shrieked.

Wendy's wet and matted hair popped through the swirling vortex, followed by her shoulders and arms.

"Get her! GET HER NOW!" the lawyer cried.

Joey swung back onto the cable and reached for the harness latch. Suddenly, the A-frame twisted and fell, toppling in the direction of the truck. Mr. Hanson grabbed the boy just as he seized the girl. With a quick motion the teenager unlatched the harness and they all fell hard across the stone-lit-

148

tered bed of the now moving vehicle. With a grinding snap, the frame collapsed and sank into the churning water. In horror, the men at the tree line saw the front of the truck rise as the back end began to slide into the widening hole from which Joey and Wendy had just emerged.

"Oh, MY!" Ranger Perez exclaimed, not believing what he was seeing. "The river's trying to suck them back into the opening!"

Joey, Wendy, and Mr. Hanson felt their world tilt violently. Piles of neatly stacked rocks slipped from the truck bed, knocking the trio down as they tried to stand. The lawyer grabbed the vehicle's roll bar and wrapped his legs around Joey, who caught hold of Wendy's harness. As the truck's front tires continued to rise, they saw the rocks slide out of the bed with a rumbling screech and disappear into the swirling currents circling the hole.

"I . . . can't . . . hold . . . on," Joey groaned, feeling his grip on the harness begin to slip. "Wendy! Let the . . . animal . . . go."

"No!"

"I . . . can't hold . . . you both."

"He'll die!"

The truck lurched sideways, tilting awkwardly, throwing its three passengers sharply to the right. The winch broke from its bolts and brushed past them, vanishing without a sound into the vortex.

"Wendy!" Joey moaned. "It's . . . too much. I can't hold . . . on."

"You promised," the girl sobbed. "You promised

you'd save him, too."

Joey felt the harness jerk out of his palms and catch in his bent, trembling fingers. The girl was right. He had promised.

With all the strength he could muster, Joey gave one final try. Slowly, painfully, he began lifting the girl and mountain lion toward him. Inch by inch his burden rose, higher and higher into the truck bed, away from the whirlpool that spun dizzily just below Wendy's riding boots. The boy ground his teeth, straining with the effort, crying out above the roar of the river.

The truck lurched again, slamming him against the bed.

"Come on, Joey," Mr. Hanson pleaded, suddenly understanding what the boy was trying to do. If the three of them could position themselves high enough on the truck, the vehicle's front end might drop slightly, making it easier to maneuver.

Sure enough, as Wendy's weight continued to rise, the truck responded by dropping its front tires back toward the rapids. Wendy kicked out repeatedly, finally finding a toehold, providing a bit of help to the boy who strained to lift her.

Ranger DeMitri realized he hadn't taken a breath for more than a minute. "Look!" he gasped. "The front of the truck's dropping back into the water. Praise God. Praise God in heaven!"

Mr. Perez glanced over at his friend. "I didn't know you were a religious man."

The ranger grinned broadly. "You gotta start

sometime. This moment seemed appropriate."

Mr. Hanson felt the vehicle settle and heard the currents rushing past, shaking the truck in its powerful grasp. He looked down at his daughter and Joey. "Are you two OK?" he called.

The girl opened her eyes and loosened her death grip on the mountain lion. The cat blinked a couple times and stared nose to nose at his friend. Water dripped from hair and fur. "I think Monty is scared," Wendy announced.

Joey rolled over onto his back and gasped for air. After a moment, he lifted himself up on one elbow and peered over the edge of the truck bed at the churning currents sweeping by. "Oh, this is much better," he said.

The truck shifted again, throwing its passengers to one side.

"How we gonna get to shore?" the boy asked, trying to find a handhold. "I don't know how long this old jalopy'll stay upright in the middle of the river. We've gotta get outta here."

The lawyer shook his head. "Seems like we just keep jumping out of the frying pan into the fire. I think that's how Grandpa would describe this situation."

"What we need now is a good pair of wings," Wendy breathed.

A smile began to play on Mr. Hanson's face. "Will those do?" he asked, pointing skyward.

Hawk banked the Pacemaker sharply to the right, glancing down his wing to the incredible sight below. He could see the truck and the frightened passengers hanging on for dear life in its about-to-be-submerged bed. But what filled him with the most dread was the view of the river. It was angry. He could tell. Years of observing earth from sky had taught him many of the peculiarities of nature. That's why he knew he was looking at a river seemingly driven by an emotion, an almost human sentiment of frustration and wrath.

Brushing the unsettling image from his thoughts, he began calculating the approach to the water, factoring in the speed of the current and the small spaces available to him. It would be close. Very close.

"I'm going in," he radioed to base camp, the microphone held tightly in his hand.

"Roger, Tiger One. Hold your fire until passing 500."

Hawk blinked. The landscape was filled with craters. Trees stood bent, broken, and shattered, still smoking from earlier attacks.

"I can't do it," the man shouted. "I can't do it anymore."

"Tiger One, arm your Mavericks now. Do you read? Switch on your tracking camera before firing."

"No."

"Wait for target verification before releasing your salvo. Make this one count, Hawk."

"NO!" The pilot's hands shook at the controls. He could hear the arming mechanisms clicking on somewhere in the aircraft. He could feel the Gforces sinking him deeper into the seat, his pressure suit inflating about his stomach and chest in an attempt to keep the blood from flowing out of his head.

"I can't. I CAN'T!"

"Fire on my mark, Tiger One, in five . . . four . . . three . . ."

The man screamed, years of buried guilt lifting his cry. "I won't do it. I WON'T!"

"Two . . . one . . . Fire. Fire! Fire!"

"I . . ." Hawk shouted as he slammed the control stick back against his seat.

"AM . . ." He felt the aircraft shake as it arched through the sky.

"FORGIVEN!" The Pacemaker rose from its dive and roared upward, engine shrieking at full power. The vision was gone, and for the first time, Hawk felt at peace in the air, at peace with himself. It was a sensation he knew he'd never lose again.

"Looks like he's comin' around for another try," Mr. Hanson called, pointing.

Above the trees, at the far end of what used to be an open meadow, the airplane moved into position, pointed straight at the truck. The passengers saw the planer turn a bit to the side, then straighten out again, losing altitude rapidly.

"OK, Hawk," the pilot said aloud, his voice firm and steady. "Here's your chance to start *saving* lives. Don't mess up. Just don't mess up. You can do it. I know you can do it."

The surface of the water that raced toward him

was rough. He figured he'd have just enough room to plant his floats in the rapids and stop his onward thrust before it carried him past the truck. But it would take every bit of flying skill he possessed, and maybe a little bit more.

"How 'bout it, God?" he whispered. "Would You help an old soldier who's trying to change his life? Please. I can't do it alone."

The aircraft slammed into the water in a fountain of spray. Joey and the others saw it swerve, almost digging a wing into the rapids, then right itself. With a roar, the plane lurched to a stop, then began inching in their direction, fighting the currents.

Mr. Hanson stumbled to the top of the cab, crouching hesitantly at the edge. As the bright red wing of the airplane swept over him, he took hold of the second strut, almost losing his balance in the process.

"Get in!" he shouted to Wendy and Joey as Hawk adjusted the throttle to keep the craft powered against the river's force. "You first, Wendy."

Joey helped the girl climb onto the cab of the truck, Monty still held tightly in her arms. Her father unlatched the Pacemaker's door and held it open. "Hurry, Wendy," he urged. "You've got to hurry."

The girl jumped from the truck into the plane, landing hard on the floor.

Joey tossed himself in next. He turned. "Come on, Mr. H."

The man was about to follow the others when the truck suddenly pushed away, the cab rising wildly into the air. Mr. Hanson found himself hanging from the wing strut, his feet dragging in the cold water. "Daddy!" Wendy shouted. "Hold on! HOLD ON!"

Hawk saw the truck spin and sink below the river's surface, its headlights pointing skyward. The hole had claimed another victim.

The added weight so far out on the wing caused the aircraft to turn and tilt drunkenly. Hawk pushed the throttle forward, fighting the powerful sucking action of the vortex. He saw the horizon begin to spin around as the Pacemaker edged closer and closer to the dark hole.

"Power! Full power!" he commanded. His hand shoved the throttle to the firewall as the sound of the engine rose from a roar to a scream. Just as the front of the floats began to rise, their rear ends dipping into the vortex, he felt the Pacemaker jerk forward, responding to the powerful thrust created by the spinning propeller.

"Slide down!" Joey shouted to the man dangling out of reach, halfway to the end of the wing. "Slide down, Mr. H. I'll catch you."

The man swung his legs and caught the strut with a foot. As the aircraft shuddered in midstream, he slowly slipped toward the fuselage. When his feet reached the float, Joey grabbed his belt and pulled with all his might. The lawyer lunged forward, falling into the cabin and landing with a thud on top of Joey.

"Go!" Mr. Hanson shouted above the roar of the

engine. "Go, Hawk. We're all in now!"

Hawk turned the aircraft into the wind, his feet dancing on the rudder pedals. The Pacemaker bolted forward in response to the man's control, even as Joey fought to close the door. The plane shook and trembled, fighting the waves, bouncing about as its pilot steered around submerged rocks and logs.

Hawk could feel the wings fighting for lift, trying to overcome the drag created by the floats as they slammed into wave after wave.

"Hold on," he shouted. "It's gonna be tight!"

His passengers grabbed whatever was closest and waited, breath caught in their throats. They stared at the trees that seemed to fill the forward windscreen as the man fought to keep the Pacemaker heading in the direction he must go. Then, suddenly, the pounding stopped. The floats had cleared the river.

Hauling back on the control stick, Hawk took in a breath and held it. The aircraft staggered drunkenly toward the trees, engine and propeller screaming, wings shaking.

"Here it comes!" the pilot called.

The Pacemaker's floats brushed branches and leaves, slicing some off, leaving others bent. And then they were clear, climbing unimperiled into the cool mountain air.

"We did it!" Joey shouted, pounding the seat joyfully with his fists. "The river didn't take us. We got away."

Mr. Hanson grabbed Wendy and held her close, hot tears staining his face. When he could speak, he simply repeated a thankful phrase. "My girl. My little girl."

A movement between them caused him to push away. Monty snarled and lifted a paw, claws bared. "Don't worry," Wendy said, stroking the cat's head lovingly with her dirt-stained hand. "That's just my dad. He's harmless. You'll get use to him."

Joey smiled. "Yeah, Monty," he said. "It may take a while, but he'll grow on you, just like Wendy did."

Hawk leaned his head back and called above the din of the engine. "Anybody lose a horse back there?"

Wendy's smile faded.

"Well," the man continued, "you'd better take a look. There's something out on the ridge you might be interested in."

Wendy raised herself to the window and stared down on a sweeping vista of forests and mountains. At eye level, moving slowly along the crest of a hill, was a little green vehicle heading eastward. And out in front, guided by a man with a cane, stumbled a small, brown horse, white star on his forehead.

"Early!" Wendy shouted. "Look, Daddy. Look, Joey. He's walking. Early's walking!"

The pilot pulled back on the throttle, decreasing the speed of the aircraft. "I'll fly by slowly so you can say hello," he said.

Debbie pressed on the brake and brought the Trooper to a quick stop. "Barry," she called out the window. "Look over there. It's an airplane. I think it's Hawk's."

Wrangler Barry spoke softly to the limping stallion and pulled gently on its halter. "Hold on there, boy. We may have visitors."

157

The aircraft dipped lower and lower until it was flying just beyond the edge of the mountain trail. As it swept by, the man with the horse could see a young face pressed against the back window, eyes filled with wonder and delight, lips moving slowly, forming two words he recognized immediately.

As the Pacemaker roared back into the sky, continuing its flight out of the wilderness, Barry smiled. "You're welcome, Wendy," he whispered.

Debbie checked on the sleeping form of Samantha in the back seat, then ran to join her friend on the trail. They stood watching the Pacemaker fade into the distance, racing toward the setting sun. The two were silent for a long moment, feeling the cool mountain air blowing softly past them.

"So," Barry said quietly, "whadda ya think about spending the rest of your life with a guy who can't live his dreams, but who's willing to find a place for himself in someone else's?"

Debbie pressed her cheek next to his, her heart singing with joy. "I'd like that very much, cowboy," she said softly. "As a matter of fact, I have a couple of dreams I'd be willing to share."

They stood for a few more moments there on the ridge, watching the wilderness slowly sink into evening. Dusk spread its shadowy blanket over the land, wrapping every mountain and tree in the dark folds of night. In the stillness, the only sound that could be heard was the call of the wind, and the distant roar of the river.

The Shadow Creek Ranch Series

by Charles Mills

1. Escape to Shadow Creek Ranch

Joey races through New York City's streets with a deadly secret in his pocket. It's the start of an escape that introduces him to a loving God, a big new family, and life on a Montana ranch.

2. Mystery in the Attic

Something's hidden in the attic. Wendy insists it's a curse. Join her as she faces a seemingly life-threatening mystery that ultimately reveals a wonderful secret about God's power.

3. Secret of Squaw Rock

A group of young guests comes to the ranch, each with a past to escape and a future to discover. Share in the exciting events that bring changes to their troubled lives.

4. Treasure of the Merrilee

Wendy won't talk about what she found in the mountains, and Joey's nowhere to be found! Book 4 takes you into the hearts of two of your favorite characters as you see events change their lives forever.

5. Whispers in the Wind
Through the eyes of your friends at the ranch, experience the worst storm in Montana's history and a Power stronger than the fiercest winds, more lasting than the darkest night.

6. Heart of the Warrior
The deadly object arrives without warning. Suddenly Joey realizes he's about to face the greatest challenge of his young life. He's answered threats like this before. But never from an Indian.

7. River of Fear
A horse expedition brings Joey and Wendy face-to-face with the terrifying results of sin. Wendy goes for help but soon finds herself in more trouble than anyone else.

Each paperback is US$5.95, Cdn$8.65 each. Look for more books in the series coming soon.